"So I guess we're even, huh?"

Nikki leaned forward to set down her cup on the cocktail table. Her robe gaped open as she did so, and Adam's gaze fell straight to her spectacular breasts.

Noticing where his attention was, she put her hands up to tug the edges of the robe together.

"Please don't," he asked softly.

She swallowed, hesitating. Then, blushing furiously again, she tugged the lapels of the robe *open*. And then, to his stunned disbelief, she removed the pasties on her nipples and let her breasts spill out to greet him.

The air went out of him so fast that his lungs almost collapsed. His mouth gaped open like a grouper's.

D cups. Perfect, high and round and cherry-capped. *Fair?* No, this was incredibly *un*fair. Because Adam wanted to touch them in the worst way. His palms itched, he wanted them so badly. He was afraid he was going to start panting like a dog.

He was crazy; he shouldn't have brought her here.

Blaze

Dear Reader,

Over the years, we've all read stories about brides, grooms and bridesmaids. One day a thought came to me. I couldn't recall ever reading romances that revolved around those *other* hot guys in tuxedos at a wedding: the groomsmen!

And so the idea for my series All the Groom's Men was born. I decided that the first book would begin at the groom's bachelor party, and I started making notes. Out of nowhere came an image: a girl exploding out of a cake and knocking one of the bachelors to the floor.

The heroine of this book, *Borrowing a Bachelor,* was very clear in my mind. She wasn't a professional dancer—she was an *accidental* stripper, someone who had taken a one-time gig out of financial duress. And the hero told me that he didn't want to be at the party in the first place....

I hope you enjoy reading about the misadventures of Nikki and Adam as much as I enjoyed writing them! I love hearing from readers, so let me know. Feel free to email me at Karen@KarenKendall.com, and check my website www.KarenKendall.com for upcoming stories, contests and more!

Have a great year filled with joy and good books!

All the best,

Karen Kendall

Karen Kendall

BORROWING A BACHELOR

TORONTO NEW YORK LONDON
AMSTERDAM PARIS SYDNEY HAMBURG
STOCKHOLM ATHENS TOKYO MILAN MADRID
PRAGUE WARSAW BUDAPEST AUCKLAND

Recycling programs
for this product may
not exist in your area.

ISBN-13: 978-0-373-79665-6

BORROWING A BACHELOR

Copyright © 2012 by Karen Moser

This edition published by arrangement with Harlequin Books S.A.

For questions and comments about the quality of this book
please contact us at Customer_eCare@Harlequin.ca.

® and TM are trademarks of the publisher. Trademarks indicated with
® are registered in the United States Patent and Trademark Office, the
Canadian Trade Marks Office and in other countries.

www.Harlequin.com

Printed in U.S.A.

ABOUT THE AUTHOR

Karen Kendall is the author of more than twenty novels and novellas for several publishers. She is a recipient of awards such as the Maggie, the Book Buyer's Best, the Write Touch and *RT Book Reviews* magazine Top Pick, among others. She grew up in Austin, Texas, and has lived in Georgia, New York and Connecticut. She now resides in south Florida with her husband, two greyhounds, a cat…and lots of fictional friends! Of course, she claims to have real ones, too.

Books by Karen Kendall

HARLEQUIN BLAZE
195—WHO'S ON TOP?*
201—UNZIPPED?*
207—OPEN INVITATION?*
246—MIDNIGHT OIL†
252—MIDNIGHT MADNESS†
258—MIDNIGHT TOUCH
333—MEN AT WORK
    "Through the Roof"

*The Man-Handlers
†After Hours

Other titles by this author available in eBook

With thanks to Young Royce for the information
on medical school courses and texts!
xo, Karen

1

MEDICAL STUDENT ADAM Burke was deeply engrossed in his anatomy text when a size-twelve foot kicked it out of his hands. It flew up and banged him in the chest.

"Pull your head out, nerd! We have a bachelor party to go to. Ogling strippers is a much better way to study anatomy."

Adam hated strip joints—the cheesiness of them and the overpriced drinks, just for starters. He groaned. "Devon, I have a killer exam on Monday. And it's not on the finer points of silicone implants."

"All work and no play will turn your hair prematurely gray," Devon said, seizing the twenty-pound anatomy book and tossing it onto the king-size bed in their hotel room.

"No, *you* will. Where did you come from, anyway?" Adam frowned and then belatedly noticed the open door.

Devon followed his gaze and laughed. "Good detective work, Holmes. I can't believe you didn't hear me come in—you're scary intense when you study."

That was true—though there had been a time in

high school, when he'd been "in love" with the class bad girl, during which Adam had been just as intense about screwing off to impress her. He'd tried his best to mess up his life.

"I have to be. You don't get into, or through, med school without the ability to focus." Adam, now twenty-five, ran a hand through his hair and reluctantly got up from the armchair he'd been sitting in. "Bachelor party, huh?" He said it without a trace of enthusiasm.

"Fire up, buddy. Mark's getting married—going over to the Dark Side. We're the groomsmen. We gotta send him off in style, with lots of drinks and lots of well-endowed women."

Adam saw the glint in Devon's eye. It told him that protesting would do no good. His only hope was to go to the damned party and wait the requisite hour or so until all the guys were so shit-faced that they wouldn't notice him sneak out. He really didn't have time for this.

Devon started to describe the various abilities of the "talent" that awaited them. "They've got this one chick who walks around with a selection of cigars tucked in her G-string. You get a lap dance while you choose one. Then another girl will hold your cigar for you between her hooters while girl number three bends over and lights it with a match between her teeth."

"I can't wait," said Adam without a trace of sincerity.

"And that's just the beginning. This place we're going gets wild. Later, this other chick, the star attraction, will take it *all* off and do things that you can't even imagine. She's got a prehensile—"

"Enough. I get the picture."

"No, really, she can pick up a lit cigar from an ashtray with her—"

"Gross. Dev—"

"—and bring it up to your mouth again. I once saw a guy—"

"Devon! *Enough.* And do you have any idea how unsanitary that is?"

"Dude. I'm not saying I'd smoke it again myself, just that it was a trip to watch."

Blek. Adam would rather have a root canal. Not that he didn't like naked women. But he liked them a little more wholesome than that. He wasn't a fan of strippers and blatant womanly wiles. The whole scene was so far removed from his daily life, where most of the females he encountered wore either sweats, jeans or surgical scrubs—not fishnets or pasties.

Adam also didn't care for most of the men who hung out at these clubs. They were generally either creeps or assholes. After they left the clubs, it wasn't unusual for the former to use their fists to abuse themselves and the latter to use their fists to abuse others. Emergency rooms were full of bruised and bloody idiots who had limped out of bars.

"C'mon, c'mon," Dev urged him. "You got ten minutes to grab a shower and pull yourself together."

"I am together," said Adam, looking at Devon's spiky, product-laden hair and the chain around his neck. He looked like some kind of designer dog. "And at least I don't have grease in my mop like some others I could mention. You're the one who needs the shower. Also, if you're going to wear a choke chain, where's your rabies tag?"

"Grease? This is *Pomade à l'Hommes,* imported from

Paris, and it costs a mint, thank you very much. I'm
going to ignore your gratuitous comment about my—"

"*Pomade a l'*homosexual, more like," Adam said,
grinning.

"Dude. You know better. I scored with number
three hundred and twenty-six last month. That's a lot
of women since age fourteen…"

"Yeah. It makes me wonder when your dick's gonna
fall off and what you're trying to prove." Adam disappeared into the bathroom, ignoring the insults Devon
hurled at him through the door. Devon didn't have a
gay bone in his body, but it was fun to rile him.

The quick hot shower cleared Adam's brain of fog
and snapped him awake, since the anatomy text had
had a sedative effect in spite of his legendary focus. He
wrapped the hotel towel around his waist and shaved,
though he didn't know why he bothered.

Then he threw on his clothes, cracked his knuckles
like a caveman and girded his decidedly *not* inflamed
loins for the evening.

NIKKI FINE STARED AT the huge, hollow plywood cake
on wheels in front of her. It was frosted with spackle
and house-paint in unfortunate shades of peach and
blue, and it had seen better days. Scuffs and footprints
marred the once-festive surface, and a big chunk of
icing had chipped off one side.

She shook her head. "I can't get in there," she
said. "I'm claustrophobic and I'm afraid of the dark."
Nobody had told her she'd be wheeled into the bachelor
party this way. The inside of the cake might as well be
a coffin as far as she was concerned. And was that a
spiderweb down there? She shivered involuntarily.

Nikki always kept a tiny light plugged in next to

her nightstand. Rationally she knew that there were no monsters under her bed. She was an adult, after all. But somehow she'd never outgrown her fear of total blackness in a room. And lately she'd had recurring nightmares about being buried alive after seeing a news story on the modus operandi of a particularly charming serial killer.

She was not getting into that small round box. No way.

Her neighbor Yvonne Morales blinked at her, tossing her glossy dark mane over her shoulder. Then she laughed. "Get over it, chica. You've been *hired.* Climb into the damn cake."

"I can't," Nikki said for the third time.

Not even in the name of paying off her crushing debt could she get in there.

"You want to lose this job in the first hour you have it? What about all that whinin' you did about being broke and needing to pay the minimum on your credit cards? What's your problem?"

Nikki gulped. *Small, dark places. That's my problem. And total fear that I'm going to make an idiot out of myself in front of a hundred guys. Who was I kidding? I can't moonlight as a stripper.* "Look," she said to Yvonne. "I kind of exaggerated my dancing skills. I can't dance at all. I didn't even make pep squad in high school." In fact, she'd been mocked by the mean girls for even attempting it.

Hey, Nikki, you're so fine, you're so fine, hey, Nikki!

She pushed aside the painful memory and the chorus line of the song they'd used to torment her. How she'd hated her name back then.

Yvonne laughed. "You don't gotta dance. You pop the top off the cake and wiggle around. Then pop your own top. The dumb-asses in the bar are all drunk, anyway. They couldn't tell the difference between you and Britney Spears out there. Just shake it and smile and lick your lips a lot."

The more she thought about it, the more Nikki realized exactly how bad an idea this was. "What if someone I know recognizes me?"

"In ten pounds of stage makeup, false eyelashes and pasties? I really don't think so. And believe me, they will not be focused on your face."

No, they would be focused on her breasts and her booty. No secret there. She flushed with humiliation as she remembered her experience at Yvonne's waxing place.

C'mon, honey, we got to get you a Brazilian before tomorrow if you're goin' onstage in a G-string.

Nikki had had to take off all clothing—*all*—below her waist. Then she'd been ordered onto a platform table and told to spread 'em while a strange woman had smacked noisily on her gum and stared at what Yvonne would call her "box."

Not only had the strange woman stared at it, she'd snipped at it with small scissors and then spread hot wax in highly embarrassing places with a wooden tongue-depressor. Far worse, she'd pressed muslin strips into the wax and then—

"Oww!" Nikki had shrieked.

The woman snapped her gum and rolled her eyes as she tossed the strip into the trash. Then she grinned evilly and grasped another.

Approximately seventeen yelps later, her tormentor had made her roll over and assume an even more horrendous position.... Nikki closed her eyes simply thinking about it. She'd refused to speak to Yvonne once she emerged from the chamber of horrors, while her neighbor just laughed and laughed.

Nikki had raced home, submerged her lower half in a tub of cold water, clamped her knees and gulped a glass of wine without stopping to breathe. Then she'd poured another and popped four painkillers.

This morning the angry red bumps had faded to a nice pink blush, a perfect background for the tiny heart that now nestled at the apex of her legs. *I am a fallen woman,* Nikki thought. *Now, do I really need to pop out of a cake and fall again? Right on my butt in front of a bunch of horny, drunken men?*

No, I do not. Best to walk away from this cake and this terrible job and figure out a different way to pay my credit cards.

The balance on the cards haunted her and made her want to puke when she thought about it. And it wasn't from irresponsibility, either—who could have foreseen that a perfectly healthy twenty-four-year-old would fall victim to appendicitis right after losing her job and declining to pay the huge hike in fees for COBRA?

It seemed beyond unfair. But she was the one who had been dumb enough to borrow money last month from Yvonne…to tide her over until her new job started.

Yvonne grasped Nikki by the upper arms and shook her—not so gently. "Get a grip, girlfriend. I put myself on the line for you. You can't back out now or I'm gonna look bad and my manager will blame me when these guys call and complain. I do not need that, and I don't have time to get somebody else over here to cover this event. So you move your little *culo* and climb into that cake before I slap you into next month."

Nikki stiffened in surprise. Yvonne's tone wasn't

so friendly and lighthearted anymore. Neither were Yvonne's fingers as they dug into her flesh. And her eyes—they'd hardened to the point of glassiness.

Nikki should have known better than to trust a woman who'd succumbed to Miami's latest in cosmetic surgery trends and gotten butt implants.

That friendly neighbor who had become a neighborly friend? She'd turned into Tonya Harding with PMS. What had Nikki gotten herself into?

"Do it," Yvonne ordered, in a menacing voice. She looked utterly capable of going after Nikki's knees with a tire iron.

That, combined with the fact that she *had* committed to tonight's job, persuaded Nikki to raise her left foot in its ridiculously high spike heel and swing it over the edge of the wooden cake.

"Good girl," said Yvonne.

Nikki refused to look at her. *Good girl? I am dressed like a hooker and I'm walking around with a Brazilian.* She straddled the edge of the cake and peered around, looking for any sign of the occupant of that spiderweb. Nothing with beady little eyes or more legs than her stared back.

Nikki swallowed hard.

"C'mon already," Yvonne said, wearing a look of contempt and little else herself. She grabbed Nikki by the ankle that still dangled outside the wooden cake and shoved it in, knocking her off balance.

Nikki lurched and clutched wildly at the walls, finally sliding down into a nervous crouch. Her rear end felt unnaturally exposed and the G-string gave her a fierce wedgie that she didn't have room to fix.

No spider, no spider, no spider, she repeated to herself. *Nothing to be afraid of. Thirty seconds, a couple of minutes at most, then you'll be wheeled into the party and you'll jump out on cue. Breathe evenly. You can do this. Just for one night.*

Because this was the last night, the only night, that she'd humiliate herself this way. Monday she started her new job. And she would deliver pizzas on the side, do data entry at night, sell cosmetics—whatever it took. She'd pay off her cards somehow. But not like this.

"I'll be hanging in Ralph's office," Yvonne said. Ralph, her cousin, owned the strip club. "You can come get paid afterward."

She shook her head as she stared unblinkingly at Nikki. "You're actually scared. That's pathetic. Get a smile on your face this second. Now, head down."

Nikki produced a smile as genuine as a Vuitton bag on a New York street-vendor's cart and bent forward. Then everything went terrifyingly black and airless as the lid crashed into place.

ADAM TRIED TO LOOK as enthusiastic as the other raucous, on-their-way-to-drunk guys at Mark's bachelor party. He waved a beer around and even did a couple of tequila shots, but inwardly he sighed.

The only good thing about his rebel year in high school was that it had gotten the partying mostly out of his system—and then he'd had to pay a steep price to get his life back together. Not even the local junior college had wanted him until his persistence wore down the admissions people. He'd finally been able to transfer to a state university's pre-med program, but only after two years of a solid 4.0 GPA.

He cast a surreptitious glance at his watch, making plans to sneak out and spend a passionate night back at the hotel with his anatomy text. And he cheered wildly and made ape noises with the rest of them as a bouncer wheeled in a giant, shopworn "cake."

Mark's round cheeks had flushed with alcohol, which turned his naturally ruddy complexion a dark red. His short, curly hair stuck up in tufts, courtesy of all the headlocks and noogies the guys had inflicted. He gazed at the cake expectantly, and the others moved like a herd to stand around the front of it.

Derek made coyote noises, as if he were howling at the moon. Pete grinned his good-natured, Mr. Customer Service grin and waited patiently. Gib stood, bowlegged as he always did, looking as though he'd produce a rope and lasso the girl as soon as she emerged. Jay lounged with his hands in his pockets, eyes almost crossed. He was probably writing a murder mystery in his head.

Adam rolled his own eyes and stepped around to the back of the wooden cake, since he figured watching their expressions would be a lot more fun than watching the skanky chick who'd jump out of it.

Joe Cocker's "You Can Leave Your Hat On" suddenly blared from the speakers in the room. How original. Adam turned an amused gaze toward Mark's face and waited.

Then the top of the plywood confection exploded off. Adam had a brief impression of golden corkscrew curls and a gorgeous, smooth ass in a hot red G-string before a feminine elbow slammed into his nose. Pain seared him between the eyes, and his glasses damn near embedded into his forehead. Adam lurched backward from the impact, sliding through a pool of some spilled drink. The next thing he knew, he was on the floor, with something cold and sticky seeping through his pants.

"Oh, God!" A distressed feminine voice floated down to him. "I *knew* something like this would happen!"

Was this a nightmare or a dream? Despite the pain, Adam registered that delectable ass again, facing him as she clambered out of the stupid cake, on legs that seemed to reach all the way to heaven. Funny how heaven looked a lot like the satin string that disappeared between her cheeks.

Correction. Heaven looked a lot like the barely restrained breasts that now swiveled toward him and bounced as she tottered over on her ridiculously high heels.

Adam's eyes widened as she bent over him and dangled the breasts like ripe, luscious fruit above his face.

"I'm so, so, so sorry!" she said. "I *told* Yvonne I was claustrophobic. I told her not to make me get in there. Are you *okay?*"

He blinked. The guys were all falling over themselves laughing—especially Mark. Only Pete, Mr. Customer Service, called out—between knee-slaps—the same question. Was he okay?

Adam gazed up at the spectacular breasts again. And like a gift from the universe, they lowered closer to his face as he lay prone. "Yeah. I'm okay," he said weakly, eyes glued helplessly to them.

The breasts heaved, and a sigh of feminine relief wafted down to him in the form of sweet, minty breath. "Oh, thank goodness. I was afraid I'd killed you."

Manfully, Adam looked away from her breasts and focused instead on her face, which was a mistake, since he found himself drowning in her large,

seawater-green eyes. Not even the fact that she wore
awful false eyelashes and cauldron-black liner could
change the loveliness of those eyes or the shocked concern they expressed.

Adam gingerly put a hand up to his nose to confirm
that it was still there, and hadn't been knocked through
the backside of his skull. His hand came away bloody,
and Cake Girl winced.

"I'm *so, so* sorry," she said again, and to his con-
sternation she burst into tears. Fat, heavy drops rolled
down her cheeks, gathering mascara and makeup in
their wake.

"Really, it's okay," Adam told her, struggling up
onto his elbows. Her tears began to plop onto his head,
and her distress grew.

"I'll take you to the emergency room right away!
You could have a concussion. Oh, God, why did I ever
think I could do this? I should have known that if I
tried to dance in public I'd murder someone."

"I'm not dead," Adam reassured her. But he almost
had a heart attack as she straddled him in the high
heels and then crouched down to take his face between
her small, soft hands. She peered intently into his eyes,
now raining black, inky tears onto his face.

They left pale white streaks down her heavily
made-up face and he didn't think he'd ever seen someone so beautiful look quite so pathetic. She sniffed
woefully.

Of course, the rest of the guys could see nothing
but their evening's entertainment hovering provocatively over him. They leered enviously at the picture
Adam and Cake Girl made, eyes fixated on her luscious bottom with its disappearing G-string. For some

reason that bothered him. Vaguely, he noticed Dev snapping pictures with his cell phone.

"I've never done this before," the girl sobbed.

Poor thing. She was truly upset. "What," he teased. "You've never coldcocked a man before? It's fun. See?"

"Of course I've never—" Briefly, she looked indignant. "What I meant was that I've never, um, stripped before. And I don't know how to do it properly, and because of that I've hurt you—but I had to get out of there. I just had to! I was coming unglued."

Adam struggled to sit up more, which brought him nose to, er, nipples. Or two inches of shadowy cleavage, depending on which way he looked. She removed her hands from his cheeks and moved back self-consciously.

"Well, I can assure you that none of the men here want you to strip properly." He winked. "They'd much rather you did it improperly."

Her lush mouth worked for a moment. Then she stood so that his eyes now met her— Oh, *Christ.* A tiny scrap of satin covered it, and it looked so sweetly beckoning. His mouth went dry and he averted his gaze.

She grabbed a handful of cocktail napkins and brought her breasts back to eye-level as she crouched again and gently held the napkins to his nose. "What can I do to make this up to you?"

Oh, honey. Don't you know better than to ask a man that question? Adam swallowed with difficulty and tried yet again to reassure her. "Really, it's okay. Calm down."

"It's not okay. I can't calm down. And Yvonne is going to kill me now for sure. In the first hour of my employment." She put a hand over her mouth as a thought occurred to her and she gazed at him in horror. "Oh, my God. You're not going to sue me, are you?"

Adam shot her a wry grin. *No, suing was not what I had in mind, sweetheart. But it rhymes.*

He shook his head, which was a big mistake, since it made his nose throb like crazy.

"But I shouldn't even be thinking about me. Come on. We need to go straight to the emergency room. You could be seriously injured, could have a concussion—"

"From a blow to the *nose?*" Adam laughed.

"Anything's possible. My friend Becca once ran smack into a stop-sign pole because, you know, she was talking to someone over her shoulder? And she knocked herself out cold. So please, please, please let me take you to a doctor and make sure you're okay."

Her agitation was almost endearing. Adam finally made it to a full sitting position and reiterated that he was fine.

"C'mon, darlin'!" Gib bellowed drunkenly. "Show us what you've got! Shake it. Somebody start the music again."

"Emergency room," she pleaded, her eyes locked on Adam's and strangely intense.

"But I don't need—"

"Please," she said piteously.

"But—"

She leaned forward and whispered, "Don't make me get out there and dance. I can't do it tonight. I just can't. I'll throw up."

Her breasts nestled against his chest and her lush lips moved inches from his own. Adam felt the room begin to spin as all the blood in his body rushed south from his throbbing nose to his groin. His willpower spiraled down with it.

"Please," she said again. "I'll make it worth your while. I'll dance privately, just for you...."

Only a complete pig would take advantage of this situation and exploit the poor woman, Adam's big head told him.

Too bad he was now listening to the little head. *She broke your nose, dude. And she's a stripper. She does this a lot, no matter what she says. Why not have a private dancer, just for tonight?*

Adam got to his feet, conscious of the fact that because of the spilled drink on the floor, he looked as if he'd messed his pants. He pretended to be dazed. "Guys," he said. "I'm sorry, but I need to have my head examined."

2

Nikki felt a rush of gratitude as she and her victim helped each other to stand. "I'll drive him to the emergency room," she said to the boys. "I'm the one who knocked him down." But her gratitude turned quickly to alarm as she and Bloody Nose were surrounded by a wall of drunken, denim-clad testosterone and various expressions of male disappointment.

The consensus was that she, Nikki, had a job to do and she wasn't going anywhere until she'd done it to their satisfaction.

"You gonna load him up into that cake, darlin'?" mocked the bowlegged guy who'd yelled for her to start dancing again. "It's obviously made for the autobahn."

Nikki bit her lip. "No, of course not. My car's outside," she said, turning to Bloody Nose. And she couldn't wait to get into it, before Yvonne caught her and disemboweled her for screwing up the gig. "By the way, what's your name?"

"Adam," he said. "What's yours?"

"Nikki."

"Is that short for Nikita, female assassin?"

"No," she said, flushing. "It's short for plain old Nicole."

"*Plain* and *old* are not adjectives that I'd use to describe you," said Adam, wincing as he examined the blood-soaked cocktail napkins.

Nikki grabbed another handful, extended them to him and looked into the steady brown eyes behind their wire-rimmed glasses. She wondered which adjectives he *would* choose. But she didn't have the nerve to ask. *Clumsy* and *moronic* might be among them. Or *slutty*. She needed her street clothes and purse, but she was petrified of running into Yvonne.

"I'll drive you to the E.R., Adam," said a cheerful-looking dark-haired guy who reminded her of a teddy bear. "Leave the talent here for everyone else to enjoy."

Adam shot the guy an evaluative look. "Pete, you couldn't drive a Big Wheel right now. You've had half a bottle of tequila. But thanks."

"I got you covered." Another member of the bachelor party pushed his way forward, this one with a gold chain around his neck and enough gel in his hair to grease down a Siberian husky.

Adam outright laughed. "We took a cab here, Devon. Remember?"

Devon stopped talking midprotest and looked sheepish. Then he said, "I'll drive Pete's car."

"No way," Adam said. "Who here hasn't had at least four or five drinks already?"

The bowlegged guy squinted and started counting on his fingers. The one Adam had called Pete turned redder than he already was, and the groom burped sheepishly.

"That's what I thought," Adam said. "I'm the only sober one here—apart from Nikki. So I'm afraid, gentlemen, that the talent comes with me." He put his arm protectively around her shoulders, and she could have kissed him.

Pete frowned as he swayed back and forth, looking owlish. "No, no, no. Talent gotta stay. I have a cell phone!"

"Congratulations," Adam told him.

Pete blinked. "Thank you." He hiccupped. "I have a cell phone, so I can call a cab. To take you to the 'mergency room. C'mon, bro. Talent stays."

Horrified, Nikki looked at Adam to see if he had an answer for that one. He didn't seem to.

"Wait!" she said. "The talent should go...because I *have* no talent. Really!" Not to mention the issue of that jumbo bag of M&M's she'd eaten yesterday. She was sure that they'd already adhered in sugary little lumps all over her hips and backside.

But the idiots didn't seem to be listening. They stood gawking at her as if her breasts were two NFL announcers debating the last play at the Super Bowl—and they each had a thousand bucks riding on the outcome.

The bowlegged guy they'd called Gib said hoarsely, "We don't care about talent, sweetcakes. Just get out there and wobble around for us. Shake it like you mean it."

Nikki gulped and looked at Adam. "Please get me out of here," she mouthed. "I'll make it up to you."

"Guys," he said, "let her drive me. I'll pay for the next round and I'll get you *two* other strippers. Just let me take this one." He dug some cash out of his pocket and slapped it into Gib's hand.

The general consensus among those who could still employ rational thought was that two was better than one, and free booze wasn't something to be turned down. So, feeling a little like a piece of traded live-stock, Nikki tiptoed into the dressing room behind the stage, thankful that there was no sign of Yvonne. She fell on her belongings like a vulture, not even taking the time to dress, and scrambled out as fast as she could.

Then she took Adam's arm and tottered toward the door with him. She'd bet her feet in the high heels hurt almost as much as his nose.

The humid South Florida air washed over her nearly naked body as they left the bar. She inhaled the scents of auto exhaust, sweetly decaying vegetation and fast food, but none of them made her feel as sick as the idea of dancing in there for the wolf-whistling, howling crowd of men.

"Thank you," she said to Adam.

"No, no. Thank *you*," he said. Oddly, he seemed to mean it.

She flushed. "I'm really sorry that I've ruined your good time."

"You didn't. I hate those places. Cheap booze, cheap wo—" He broke off, but she knew he'd been about to say *cheap women*.

She looked down at her current get-up and couldn't really argue. Only the vitals were covered, and just to remind her of it a stinging insect bit her on the backside. "Ow!" Nikki exclaimed, slapping at it.

Behind the cocktail napkins, Adam's eyes widened slightly, and he swallowed hard, averting them.

"I'd offer to pay for the, um, other talent and the round of drinks," she said, "but I'm dead broke, which is why I even considered doing this."

"Don't worry about it," said Adam.

She led the way to her car, a powder-blue Volkswagen Beetle. "Where's the nearest E.R.? Or minor emergency center? Do you know?"

"I'll be fine. Really."

Nikki looked at him doubtfully. "What if I broke your nose?"

"I don't think it's broken."

"But it could be. And I've heard of all kinds of freak things that can happen—a bone fragment could pierce something in your brain, and boom! You'd be a vegetable." She shuddered.

Adam laughed. The sound was reassuring but also annoying—he wasn't taking her seriously. He was treating her like the dumb blonde she appeared to be.

"I'm serious. Look, you're not a doctor," she said in reasonable tones.

He cocked an eyebrow at her but didn't argue.

"So why don't we make sure that you're okay?" she prodded.

"Not necessary. They'll tell me to elevate the nose, keep an ice pack on it and take a couple of ibuprofen for the swelling. If a shard of bone had pierced my brain, I wouldn't be standing here talking to you. So really, you can drop me at my hotel."

Nikki gulped. She owed him a private dance in his hotel room, and she was none too eager to pay up. Any delay was a welcome one. "I'm sorry, but I insist that we get you checked out, if only for my peace of mind."

Adam sighed. "Fine," he said. "But it's a waste of time."

Wasting time sounded very good to her, especially if she could do it clothed. She dug her keys out of her purse and unlocked the Beetle. She opened the driver's-side door, tossed her things onto the seat and found her shirt. She slid on a bra—red, of course—pulled the shirt over her head and tugged it into place as Adam rounded the car and got into the passenger seat.

He watched her out of the corner of his eye as she held her white denim miniskirt in front of her, and she could have sworn she heard a swift intake of breath as she raised her leg to step into it. She pulled it up over her hips and buttoned it at the waist.

There. Now she felt better. She still wore the sky-scraper stilettos, but every woman in Miami wore those. Nikki tossed her purse into the backseat and slid behind the wheel. "Should I take you to Jackson Memorial?" she asked.

Adam shuddered. "No—the E.R. there will be full of gunshot wounds, auto-accident victims, ODs and God only knows what else. We'd wait all night." After some thought, he gave her the name of a minor emergency center close by, and directed her to it.

The building, not surprisingly, was regulation stucco with a standard red-tile roof. Adam signed in, and they waited in a shabby but comfortable sitting area done in blues and greens. The only other people there were a shrunken old man with a severe cough and a young couple. The wife rocked back and forth, clutching her stomach.

Nikki shot her a sympathetic glance, but the woman closed her eyes and wiped perspiration from her forehead with a paper towel.

After inspecting the faux wood tables, the utterly uninteresting plants and the dog-eared magazines perched haphazardly in a small rack, Nikki had nowhere to look but at Adam.

"Heh," she said idiotically.

He raised his eyebrows at her over the wad of blood-saturated cocktail napkins. "Did you say something?"

"No," she supplied, even more idiotically.

Silence fell between them again.

Nikki fidgeted. "So...what do you do?" she blurted, to make conversation.

"I'm a student."

"Of what?"

He dodged the question. "What do you do, Nikki? Besides, er...dancing?"

She felt a blush climbing her neck and then suffusing her face. "I told you—"

"Right. You've never done it before." His tone was polite, but the inflection of his voice indicated that the jury was still out on whether he believed her or not.

"I'm starting a new job on Monday," she announced defensively. "I'm an administrative assistant."

He nodded and adjusted the napkins slightly, peering at her from behind them. His glasses were smudged, which wasn't surprising. Lucky she hadn't broken them when she'd whacked him. "Do you like office work?"

Was he trying to reconcile the image of her filing with the image of her popping out of the cake wearing a G-string? She sighed. "It's okay. It's not what I want to do for the rest of my life, but it pays the bills and it gives me medical insurance." She'd never before realized what a crucial thing that was, even to a twenty-four-year-old in "perfect" health.

"Besides," she added, "I got appendicitis out of the clear blue, and had to have emergency surgery when I *didn't* have medical insurance. So I have huge debt from that."

He made a sympathetic noise. "What do you really want to do?"

She felt suddenly defensive. He was clearly a brainy type, a grad student going to school for something special, something focused, while she… Nikki wrapped her arms around herself and hunched her shoulders.

What she wanted most in the long run was a husband and a family, but it seemed so unhip to say that. Yet, given her childhood with a single mom and the fact that she'd never known her father, that *was* her dream: domestic bliss.

She pictured rabid feminists chasing her with pitchforks and cringed. "I don't know what I want to do, exactly…except that it involves having my own business." And she'd love to somehow help single moms like her own mother.

She pictured a small business that gave her plenty of time to spend with her children. She wouldn't be like her mom, who spent her days on her feet in a bakery and covered in flour, at the beck and call of other people.

But first, Nikki had to find and date the right guy. Meanwhile, she had to pay off her medical debt—and then there was the fact that her mom needed a new roof and had no way to pay for it. Meanwhile, Nikki's own rent and monthly bills didn't go away. How did *anyone* manage to save money, except rich doctor and lawyer types? It seemed impossible.

A nurse appeared and called Adam's name. He got up and went with her through a door to the back, while unaccountably Nikki fixed her gaze on his buns. Granted, his pants were damp and stained, so he did look a little as though he'd messed himself.

But she happened to know that the stains were her fault, that they'd come from the floor of the bar…and the wet fabric clung provocatively to the shape of his rear end.

It was an exceptional one. Sitting on it and studying a lot hadn't flattened it out at all.

"Nikki?"

In fact, it looked pretty muscular...especially as it turned to the side...

"Nikki."

"Huh?" She pulled her gaze upward, and realized that Adam had turned, along with his butt, and was saying her name.

Mortification was becoming her constant companion.

3

As HER CHEEKS CAUGHT on fire, Adam eyed her quizzically from behind the paper napkins. "I said that I should be right out."

"Great!" Nikki said brightly, and quickly picked up one of the magazines, spreading it open and holding it in front of her face.

Idiot! Idiot, idiot, idiot...

She dared to peek over the top of the magazine.

Adam's mouth had quirked, and his eyebrows had lifted at her choice of reading material.

It wasn't until he'd disappeared again that she looked at the cover: *Forbes*. Was he amused because he'd caught her staring at his ass, or because of her choice of magazine?

Why shouldn't she read *Forbes*? Okay, it was a dry financial publication, but for all he knew, she could be passionately interested not only in his buns—she squirmed with embarrassment—but in money. In fact, she *was* passionate about money, as far as making some went. Immediately.

Her gaze fell on one of the topics highlighted on the

cover: Securities and the Single Mom. Hmm… To take her mind off the fact that she still felt like a moron, she began to read.

By the time Adam came out with a blue-fabric, medically issued ice bag across his nose, Nikki had devoured the whole article and learned quite a bit in the process. There were all kinds of organizations and websites out there devoted to helping single moms not only with their finances, but with furthering their education—and she had the germ of a business idea.

The sight of her strip-assault victim brought her back to reality, though. "Are you okay?"

"Fine." He nodded. "It's not broken."

"Oh, thank goodness." She put down the magazine.

He walked over to the little window to pay what he owed for the visit, and Nikki jumped up. Did she have enough space free on her MasterCard to pay?

Oh, God. She wasn't sure. But she should make the offer. It was her moral obligation.

"Adam, let me take care of that. It's the least I can do."

"It's okay," he said. "Don't worry about it."

"I *will* worry about it," Nikki insisted, muttering a prayer to the credit gods under her breath. She gently nudged Adam aside. "Excuse me," she said to the woman behind the window, "but I'd like to take care of his visit."

Nikki handed her card to the woman with a smile, only barely refraining from tapping her nails nervously on the laminated countertop during what seemed an interminable wait.

"I'm sorry, ma'am, but it didn't go through."

Mortified, Nikki rummaged in her handbag and came up with a ten-dollar bill that she'd had earmarked for eggs, bread and milk. "Here, how about if you take this and then run the card again, for the balance?"

At this point, Adam took over. He folded both card and bill back into Nikki's hand and said, "I've got this. Thanks, but I've got it." He handed a credit card to the lady.

Nikki wished that a convenient sinkhole would open up in the floor and swallow her whole. A tic started at her left eye, though she tried to rub it away. *Loser, loser, loser,* it seemed to say.

She struggled with her desire to go home and crawl under the covers, to block out this whole evening and the ridiculous idea that she, the fat kid they'd called Chubba Bubba in grade school and mocked even more in high school, could possibly dance in front of men for money.

Was she crazy? Had Yvonne dropped something in her drink to make her agree to do it?

But unfortunately, she'd made this nice boy with the bloody nose a promise, and her mom had brought her up that only scabs didn't keep their promises.

Was it worse to be a scab than a loser? Nikki didn't want to think about that too much.

"Okay," she said to Adam once they were outside the door. "I promised you a private dance if you'd get me out of there. It's the least I can do—*ow!*" Another South Florida mosquito evidently flew up her skirt and bit her on the butt, and she slapped at it, hard.

There was an audible gulp from her male companion. "That's…not necessary," he said, as if it cost him great effort. "Don't worry about it."

For a moment she was relieved and elated. Then her conscience got her again and Nikki raised her chin. "I hit you in the nose and then I made you a promise, and

I'm going to keep it. Besides, I want to see you settled properly with your feet elevated and your head tipped back. So I'll drive you to your hotel and make sure you're comfortable…and…and then…we'll just get it over with."

Adam looked at her oddly. "You don't sound as if you want to do this, Nikki."

"What? Oh, no—I *do*," she lied.

He frowned.

"I, um—" She waved a hand. "I need the practice. Really. You'll be doing me a *favor* to watch." Okay, that was probably laying it on too thick, but Adam didn't call her on it.

"Come on. Let's stop talking and go." She teetered out to the parking lot and over to her car. She pulled on the driver's-side handle, but it was locked. Nikki fumbled her keys out of her bag and poked the relevant one toward the lock, but her hands shook and it was dark.

A couple of steps brought Adam up behind her, so close that she could smell his laundry detergent—the same brand she used—and a masculine-smelling shampoo. There was another scent that clung to Adam: faint traces of beer from the bar, but also something that reminded her of a library. Books? Paper? Ink?

"Excuse me." His arm reached around her, his hand covered hers, and with long, lean, competent fingers he inserted her key into the lock of the door, then turned it. "There," he said.

Nikki stood still for a moment, drawn to the warmth of him, the brush of his soft cotton shirt against her bare skin. She wanted to stay encircled by his arm, even lay her head against his chest. But Adam opened the car door for her, so she blinked and got in.

Adam shut the door and walked around the Beetle,

getting into the passenger side. She started the engine, and seconds later the air conditioner shot a blast of lukewarm air straight between her thighs, making her jump and squirm.

He turned his steady, chocolate-brown gaze on her once again, still holding the ice pack to his nose. "You sure you want to do this dance?"

As she looked at him, at his slightly mussed dark hair, the crinkles of good humor around his eyes, the tough jaw and the tiny indentation in his chin, Nikki found to her surprise that she did want to dance for him. She wished it were under different circumstances—after a date maybe, when they'd eaten at a nice restaurant and maybe gone to see some live music.

That wasn't the case, but she responded to his innate kindness and decency as well as his good looks. Here was a guy that she wanted to want her…and she had to meet him under *these* circumstances? She sighed inwardly, but turned her brightest smile on him.

"I absolutely do want to keep up my side of the bargain. I promised you a dance, and I'll give you one."

"It's not smart to come back to my hotel room," Adam told her. "How do you know I'm not a serial killer? A twisted rapist?"

Nikki frowned. "You don't seem like the type."

"What type would that be? They're all pretty normal-looking white guys. Most of them are married with children."

"Are you married with children?"

"Not even close, but you're missing the point."

"Are you a rapist or murderer?"

"No," he said, sounding a bit exasperated. "But you shouldn't take my word for it."

"Would you like me to check on you from my iPhone? Find out if you have an arrest record before I get out of the car?"

Adam leaned his head against the seat, adjusted the ice pack and closed his eyes. "You can't possibly be this naive."

"There's no need for name-calling," Nikki said. "I have a solution. We'll stop by the front desk at the hotel and let them know that if I'm found scattered in pieces anywhere, I spent my last hours with you. How's that?"

"Fine, laugh at me. I'm simply trying to tell you that it's a scary world out there and you shouldn't go back to strange men's hotel rooms."

"Just how strange are you?"

"I give up!"

Nikki grinned, then put the Beetle into Reverse and backed out of the parking spot. "Look, I appreciate the good advice. I really do. But I have pretty good instincts about people and my creep radar didn't go off around you."

"She has a creep radar," Adam said to nobody in particular. "Whatever that is."

Nikki laughed. "If you were a sicko, you wouldn't have tried to talk me out of going to your hotel room with you. You'd have been trying to convince me that you were the most harmless, trustworthy person on the planet. You might even have leaned on a crutch and begged for my help, Ted Bundy–style."

"Whatever," said Adam. They rode in silence for a little while.

"So you weren't having a good time at the club?" Nikki asked. "Why not?"

"Just not my scene."

"What's your scene, then?"

He shrugged. "Quiet music, smoke-free air, a beer on a back porch, watching the sunset."

"That sounds nice."

Silence fell in the car again. Nikki thought about how to dance for him. What would a guy like Adam be looking for?

"Do you have an iPod or anything for music?" she asked. She hadn't gotten around to downloading any songs on her own phone.

"Um. No, but there's a clock radio in the room."

Nikki nodded. Not ideal, but it would work in a pinch. Now…how to read him? She might as well ask.

"So," she blurted. "Do you like it fast and skanky, or do you prefer slow and sensual?"

Adam's jaw dropped. He swiveled toward her and the ice pack fell off his nose and into his lap. *"Excuse me?"* he asked, in strangled tones.

4

UNDER THE ICE PACK, Adam popped a woody. Had the girl really asked him that?

"Oh, my God!" she said. "I didn't mean that the way it came out. I meant, you know, about *dancing.*"

Adam's brain was still locked on the concept of *fast and skanky* sex, even though he tried valiantly to get rid of the images. It didn't help that the girl sitting in the driver's seat was so smoothly, er, curvilinear. Or that he'd seen her practically naked, peered either up or down every one of her female crevices.

His woody wasn't going anywhere, which was inconvenient to say the least, since they were now approaching the hotel. *Down, boy! Play dead.*

Adam really didn't want to do introductions in the parking lot. *Nikki, meet Johnson. He's enthusiastic to make your acquaintance...as you can see.*

Adam got himself under control with difficulty as he gave her somewhat convoluted directions on purpose. At last Nikki pulled into the Marriott Courtyard where he and the guys were staying.

"Didn't we just pass this?" Nikki inquired.

Adam mumbled something about being tired and forgetting to tell her to turn, but her puzzled frown told him that she didn't buy it.

Nikki opened the driver's-side door and got out, treating him to another view of her spectacular legs and ass, though he vaguely wished she hadn't felt the need to put on the skirt.

He got out as she surreptitiously scratched at one of her insect bites, and he took pity on her. "I have a first-aid kit with some cortisone cream in my room." It stayed permanently in his carry-on, and had come in handy more than once.

She nodded, her face a study in mortification under all that makeup. "Thanks." She wobbled along next to him and he took her arm to brace her as they crossed a small hillock of grass to reach the sidewalk.

Adam slid the key card through the slot at the rear door of the place, and stood aside to let Nikki enter before him. That was when he noticed the little clumps of mud and grass stuck to her spike heels. He turned his sudden laughter into a cough/snort.

Nikki turned. "Are you okay?"

"F-fine," Adam said. "Allergies." And he led the combination stripper/lawn-aerator to room 198. Another electronic snick and they walked inside.

The door closed behind them and the two of them stood there like morons, Adam looking everywhere but at her and she looking everywhere but at him. Finally he broke the silence. "I believe I promised you some cortisone cream."

"Oh, yes," she said gratefully. "And you should probably get some more ice for your nose."

He nodded.

Adam went into the bathroom and rummaged the

tube of cream out of the first-aid kit. He handed it to her, noticing that the skin of her chest and neck had flushed deep scarlet and perspiration had beaded at her temples. Clearly she was nervous. Had she really never done this before?

As she took the cap off the tube and squeezed some cream onto her finger, he retreated back into the bathroom, wet a washcloth with cold water and brought it out to her. He stopped at the sight of Nikki, twisted like a pretzel with her skirt rucked up, rubbing at the bites on her behind.

How anyone could find the sight provocative, he didn't know—he guessed he was just an unusual guy. But the position she was in elongated her neck and emphasized her curves, displaying all the lean muscle on either side of her elegant spine and the sexy flare of narrow waist into hips.

If only he could get past the indignity of what she was doing, she'd look like one of those portraits of nude bathers that he'd seen in museums. Though he doubted that Degas or Renoir had ever painted anything called *Nude with Cortisone Cream.*

"That's much better," she declared, pulling down her skirt again with a forced smile. She handed back the tube. "Thank you."

"You're welcome."

"So, I guess I'll just, um, turn on the radio…and you can get, um, comfortable."

While she gets even more uncomfortable. But Adam nodded and she teetered over to the nightstand and began to fiddle with the clock. A burst of static had both of them wincing, but Adam couldn't look away from the sight of her bent over.

"What kind of music do you like?" Nikki asked over her shoulder.

"Any rock station is fine." He swallowed hard. He remembered from the bar that she appeared to be completely hairless under that tiny thong she wore. *Completely.*

"I'm just, uh, going to go get that ice," he said in strangled tones. "Be right back."

"Okay." She looked relieved, and he wondered if she'd bolt while he was out of the room. But when he returned with some fresh ice cubes in his nose pack, she was still there, swaying awkwardly to an oldie but goodie—"Light My Fire" by the Doors.

"I can do this," she declared, as if she were trying to convince herself as well as him.

"Even with no pole, huh?" He couldn't resist teasing her a little bit.

"Oh. I forgot about the pole," she said, looking distressed.

"Don't worry about it. You can use a chair or something, right?" Adam pulled a chair out from under the room's desk and set it in the middle of the floor. Then he sat on the edge of the bed and held the ice pack to his nose.

Nikki took a deep breath, approached the chair and grasped the back. Then she began.

She gyrated her hips to the beat of the music and pressed her pink lips into a pout. After a few moments, she took the bottom of her shirt into both hands and began easing it up, teasing him with the sight of her breasts in a red push-up bra. She whipped the shirt over her head and spun around.

When she turned to face him again, she ran a hand down her smooth, flat stomach, sort of slithering it around. She played with the button at the waistband of her skirt.

The bra was the second article of clothing to go, leaving her breasts bare except for a pair of strategically placed pasties with tiny tassels that shook in every direction and betrayed her total lack of rhythm, but who cared.

She was all enticing skin and curves.

A minute or so later, she ditched the skirt, letting it drop to the floor. She stepped out of it, gyrating her hips, and kicked it to the side.

Adam's woody made a return appearance when she plunged her hand into the front of the G-string.

Adam stopped breathing at the sight.

She rotated her hips as if they were mounted on ball bearings, then leaned forward and squeezed her breasts between her arms so that they thrust forward. Then she worked her shoulders, shimmying them, too.

A cold trickle of water, followed by another one, rolled down Adam's throbbing nose and dropped onto his now equally throbbing denim-clad crotch. He was half-afraid it would start to steam.

Nikki put her hands up to her hair and pushed it on top of her head as she gyrated, letting it tumble down over her shoulders as she turned her back to him. Hot! Hot!

But then his gaze dropped again to her ass and the mosquito bites, now shiny with cortisone cream…not to mention the tufts of mud and grass on her heels. Worse, the twin mosquito bites now stared out at him from each cheek like a couple of angry red eyes.

Her thong formed two frowning eyebrows as it dipped horizontally from each hip, and the vertical part in this context looked like a nose. The cheeks were, well, cheeks. And that sweet, sweet underside as her bottom met her thighs—well, it grimaced at him.

Adam couldn't help himself—he guffawed, knowing as he did so that it was probably the worst offense he could commit.

Nikki stopped dead, her whole body stiffening in outrage.

He winced and ducked reflexively, thinking that she'd throw something at him. But it wasn't anger on her face as she turned—it was something much worse: shame. Complete and utter humiliation. And shock. And deep, deep hurt.

"Nikki—"

Shaking, she ran into the bathroom and slammed the door.

Nice, Adam. You've sure gone and done it now, haven't you? His bedside manner needed work. He groaned and walked to the door, then knocked softly. "Nikki, I wasn't laughing at you—"

"Yes, you were!" Her voice was thick with shame.

"No, not the way you think."

"I know I have no rhythm or talent and I know I'm fat," she wailed.

"Fat? Are you crazy? No, Nikki, you're not. And you do have talent…" Okay, not much, but enough to get a guy's motor running, that was for sure.

"It was the M&M's," she blurted.

"Huh?"

"Oh, God…why don't you have something in here that I can just *kill* myself with?"

Alarmed, Adam tried the knob, but she'd locked herself in. "Nikki, you can't be serious. Please, please, let me explain."

"There's nothing to explain," she wailed. "I danced and you laughed."

"It's not that simple."

"Yes, it is."

"No, no, no. Look, just give me a chance—"

"You *would* have to have an electric shaver," she said bitterly. "I can't slit my wrists with that."

"Nikki!"

"And no sleeping pills. Not even any freaking *dental floss* that I could strangle myself with."

"Nikki, don't you think you're blowing this out of proportion? I mean, even if I *had* laughed at your dancing—"

"You *did!*" This time she bellowed it.

"No, I didn't. Not the way you think." Adam ran his hands over his face, which was a mistake, since he aggravated his nose all over again. "Look. Nikki, do you have a sense of humor?"

"What?"

"I asked if you have a sense of humor."

"What do you mean?"

"If you have to ask," Adam said patiently, "then you probably don't have one."

"I do, too."

O-kay. "Then turn around and look at your, uh, bottom in the mirror."

Silence. Then, she said, "You want me to check out my own butt?"

"Yes. Just do it."

More silence. "What*ever,*" she said, in tones that indicated she was only humoring a lunatic.

Adam waited.

"Oh, my God!" she shrieked. "It looks like there's a whole face back there!"

"Exactly."

Now a definite giggle emerged from behind the bathroom door. Almost faint with relief, Adam made another suggestion. "Okay, now look at your heels."

This time she whooped.

More progress.

"I ask you," Adam appealed to her, "if you would not have laughed yourself."

Silence.

Then Nikki unlocked and opened the door, her eyes brimming with mischief and streaky makeup behind the wet washcloth she held to her flushed face. She'd pulled on the hotel's terry bathrobe.

Adam held up his hands, palms out. "Funny?"

"Funny," she confirmed, nodding.

He nodded, having absolutely no clue what to do or say next. "Listen, I feel really bad that you thought I was laughing at your dancing."

"It's okay." She scrubbed at her eyes with the cloth, only succeeding in smearing around all the black and purple goop she had on.

"Can I fix you a drink from the minibar while you take that stuff off your face? It's the least I can do to make things up to you."

She hesitated, then nodded. "A bourbon and Coke, please."

He made two of them and handed one to her when she came out. "Cheers."

"Thanks." She took a deep gulp. "How's your nose?"

"Fine. How are your mosquito bites?" He grinned.

She wrinkled her nose at him. "Fine."

"Nikki, where did you ever get the idea that you're fat?" he asked abruptly.

She tugged at the robe around her body and hugged

herself with her free arm. She took another long swallow of her drink. "Oh, you know." She shrugged.

"No, I don't know. You have a smokin' body."

"I was a really chubby kid," she blurted. "They used to call me—" She took another swallow of the bourbon and Coke, effectively finishing it off. "Never mind."

Adam took the cup from her and went to the minibar to make her another. "What did they call you?"

She picked up a guide to local attractions and thumbed through it without seeming to see anything inside.

He didn't know why he cared, but he did. "Nikki?"

"Chubba Bubba," she said, snapping the magazine closed. She shrugged again. "Stupid, huh? Really dumb that I still think about it now, at age twenty-four. But I guess it's still a sore spot."

"It's not stupid," Adam said. He gave her the second drink. "Kids can be incredibly mean."

"You have no idea," she said, taking another big gulp.

He almost advised her to take it easy, but he'd already offended her once and was unwilling to repeat the offense. "Oh, I do have a good idea. I got picked on a lot in junior high."

"Really? Why?"

He shrugged. "I was a small, nerdy kid with glasses and braces and a bad case of acne."

Surprise crossed her face. "Yeah?"

He nodded. "Yeah."

"But you're gorgeous," she blurted. Then blushed. Then gulped more of her drink.

It was his turn to blush. He felt color searing his face. He'd filled out, gone to a dermatologist and lost the braces by his sophomore year in high school. "Uh, thanks, I guess." He covered his discomfort by burying his nose in his own drink.

"I embarrassed you," Nikki said. "I'm sorry."

"Well, I laughed at your backside," Adam said. "So I guess we're even, huh?"

She dimpled and leaned forward to set down her cup on the cocktail table. Her robe gaped open as she did so, and his gaze fell straight to her spectacular breasts—what his buddy Devon would call her "luscious golden Winnebagos." The idiot.

Maybe it was the alcohol. Maybe it was temporary insanity. Or maybe—

"I'd never, ever make fun of your front side," Adam croaked, as she noticed where his gaze was fixated.

She instantly put her hands up to tug the edges of the robe together.

"Please don't," he asked softly.

She froze.

He tried a smile. "They're so beautiful. Like the rest of you."

She swallowed, hesitating. Then, blushing furiously again, she tugged the lapels of the robe *open*. And then, to his stunned disbelief, she removed the pasties on her nipples and let her breasts spill out to greet him.

The air went out of him so fast that his lungs almost collapsed. His mouth gaped open like a grouper's.

D cups. Perfect, high and round and cherry-capped. *Fair?* No, this was incredibly *un*fair. Because Adam wanted to touch them in the worst way. His palms itched, he wanted them so badly. He was afraid he was going to start panting like a dog. He was crazy; he shouldn't have brought her here. He needed to be studying for the exam on Monday. Where was his legendary hard-won focus?

"Are you okay?" Nikki asked. "Because you have a very peculiar expression on your face."

He groaned. His woody was back with a vengeance.

"Adam?"

"Look," he said. "Nikki, don't take this the wrong way…but the expression on my face is lust, pure and simple. The fact is, sweetheart, that I'd like to fu—uh, screw you into next Friday."

5

NIKKI CHOKED. *"OH!"* she said once she could manage the words. A tingle spread down her spine and intensified between her legs.

"Er," Adam responded sheepishly, looking as if he couldn't quite believe the words had come out of his mouth. "Sorry. That was probably a little uncensored."

"Yeah…but I liked it." She smiled at him.

"Did you?" He stared at her intently and then upended his drink as she nodded.

Adam set down the cup, ditto the ice pack, and got to his feet. He wiped his hands on his jeans as he crossed the carpet to where she sat; her nerves grew taut and the tingle between her legs intensified. She stopped breathing as he came to a stop in front of her.

"May I?"

Clearly, he wanted to kiss her. Nikki tilted back her head to look up at him and examined that chiseled, beautiful mouth of his. It was firm and masculine, but also sensual. His lips weren't full, but she liked the lines of them, the way they curved, the way they smiled. She imagined how those curves would fit to her own lips, fantasized about how they would feel against hers.

He bent his head, gazed into her eyes. Would he put a finger under her chin to tilt her head back? Would he take her whole face into his hands? She waited in anticipation.

But she was wrong. Adam didn't kiss her. She gasped as instead his fingers grazed her breasts. His hands were cold from the drink and the ice, but since the rest of her was inexplicably hot, the sensation was erotic.

He lifted her breasts and held them as if they were precious, then rubbed his thumbs slowly over the nipples.

She forgot all about kissing. A moan escaped her and she pushed them farther into his hands, a wordless request for more.

Adam's breathing quickened and the pupils of his eyes dilated, went darker.

Her gaze dropped from his to the formidable bulge now straining against his fly, and his hands tightened on her flesh, kneaded. He continued to tease her nipples, rubbing circles around them and flicking them gently as the sensations drove her half-crazy. Small sounds came from her throat that she couldn't control, and he seemed to like that.

"Lick them, Adam," she said. "My breasts. Please…"

He dropped to his knees between her legs, needing no further invitation. He pushed the robe from her shoulders and squeezed her breasts together, taking both nipples into his mouth at once, playing them with his tongue, and then sucking hard.

Pleasure tore a series of whimpers from her throat

and he groaned against her body, the masculine sound plucking answering strings inside her.

Adam pushed her back on the bed. He slid his hands down her body, from her breasts to her rib cage and stomach, all the way to the V of her legs, where he stopped to play a little. She sucked in a breath as those clever thumbs of his circled the damp fabric at her mons, but avoided touching her where she was wild to be touched.

He pushed her legs up onto the bed so that her heels rested at the edge, her feet dangling down. He spread her thighs and then dipped under her G-string to explore.

Nikki bucked as his fingers slid cleverly under the fabric, stroked her, and then zeroed in right below the tiny heart-shaped patch of hair.

"I have to see," he whispered, and slid the tiny panties to the side.

For a moment, there was only silence.

She lifted her head and looked through her own knees at Adam's face, which was a study in boyish awe.

"I'm gonna have a heart attack," he said in strangled tones. "Pun intended." And he stroked the little heart of hair with fascination, lust and an odd tenderness.

Her thighs quivered, and he dipped lower, slipped his fingers inside her while still manipulating the eager little nub right below the heart.

Her whole body began to shake with unfulfilled sexual tension. "Please," she whispered, hoping that he'd put his mouth on her. But how did she ask a stranger to do that?

He didn't, just as he hadn't kissed her. But he did do blissful things with his fingers, with his thumbs. She was climbing, spiraling, wanting… She lifted off the bed in a mortifying frenzy of need. "Yes," she said. "Yes…*more*. Do it. *Do* me!"

He laughed softly and obeyed.

She splintered into orgasm, losing control of her mind, her body and her dignity without caring. "Adam," she begged, "take me into next Friday, okay? Like you said."

"Oh, yeah," he breathed. "Oh, yeah." An eternity seemed to pass as he shucked out of his clothes and fumbled a condom out of his wallet. He rolled it onto the long, smooth, thick length of him.

Then he entered her in one hot, smooth stroke that left her gasping at the fullness, the sense of being possessed, the sudden different kind pleasure that streaked through her body.

She hadn't seen his cock at all, but she didn't need to, now that she felt it, now that she was deliciously impaled. He stopped only for a moment, as if to savor the act of penetrating her. Then he started to move, to pump, to groan with the pleasure of it.

She tightened around him and ran her hands up and down his back and buttocks as he stroked into her body.

"You're so hot, so hot," he murmured.

As if he had any idea. Her insides had melted into honey, and every time he slid along the cleft of her the temperature rose in streaks and flashes, liquefying her mind into her body until she was one sweet swirl of pleasure, her only focus to reach the very pinnacle of it.

He took her up, up, up…ever higher until she was saturated with his scent and his power, one with his motions and open, wide open to him. She lost herself.

And then he pitched her over the edge of climax and her body convulsed and thrashed, while she ignored the raw cries that came, uninhibited, from her throat.

Adam's big body pinned her in place as sexual pleasure radiated through her in concentric circles, his soft groans echoing her own.

Then the aftershocks eddied away, leaving them in a tangle of limbs, gasping, wondering, damp with exertion. Adam rolled off her, his only words profane and heartfelt.

"You," he said, "are…something else."

She moaned, her body still throbbing in places she didn't know it could throb. "No, you are. You made me… I mean, I—" She couldn't possibly be blushing again, could she? *"Twice."*

"Twice, huh," Adam said. He rolled toward her again. "You sound so shocked. Should we go for the magic three?"

She laughed raggedly. "I couldn't possibly. I think something fell off."

Adam propped himself up on one elbow. His hair was tousled and his mouth held a wicked curve. Lazily, he traced her nipple with a wayward finger. "You think something fell off, huh? That sounds dangerous. I'd better find it and put it back on."

Before she'd registered what he was doing, he spread her legs again and rolled between them. He took a breath and blew it out slowly on her, which was the last thing she'd expected. It tickled; it cooled her; it sent a deep shiver of pleasure through nerves that she hadn't thought could take any more. Her muscles trembled.

Clearly, he was fascinated by that tiny heart of shaven hair, because he stroked that as he blew on her again, chuckling as she squirmed.

Unbelievable, but she felt desire building in her again. If he'd touched her overly sensitive clitoris, she'd have knocked his hand away. But he didn't. He leaned closer and she could feel his warm breath as he traced the contours of the little heart. She held her breath in anticipation. Would he? Did she want him to? Any moment now, his tongue would touch her.

But it didn't.

And she did want it to.

Almost unconsciously she lifted her hips, searching for his mouth. And he chuckled again, damn him.

He slid his hands under the cheeks of her bottom and squeezed, then started to play her cleft, down low, with his thumbs. She bit her lip and pushed against them, lifted herself again and swayed.

She could feel her pulse pound all along that most private of areas, swollen from pleasure already and yet eager for more. He seemed to know. Still without touching that tiny nub at her center, he stroked the whole length of her, all the way down to her bottom.

Back and forth he trailed his fingers, and she thought she'd go crazy because it felt so good.

"You like that," he said. A statement, not a question.

"Yes," she whispered.

"You're wet for me again." His voice echoed in her ears, vibrated in her bones.

"Oh, yes…"

That's when he slipped three fingers into her. And when she whimpered, just a little, begging him for it, he at last brushed that bud at her core with his thumb, rubbing it gently until she came completely apart.

Still he didn't let up, and it became too much for her to take. "Stop…you have to stop."

"Why?"

She found his hand with her own and grabbed it. "Because I can't handle any more. I can't." She clamped her thighs together, raised her head and shoulders and looked into his eyes, which held a sweet, if smug expression. He knew he'd done his job right—done it to perfection.

"Worn you out, have I?"

She could get drunk on the cognac of his eyes. She nodded, and released their clasped hands from between her thighs. Adam freed his hand from hers and held up a specific number of fingers, still moist from her body. He waggled them at her.

"Three," he said, his voice a mixture of affection and raw, masculine desire. "Always a lucky number."

Nikki blushed. Three orgasms in a row, from a guy she'd only met less than three hours ago? Yeah…she had to admit, she'd gotten pretty lucky.

And he had, too—at least she could tell herself that as long as she didn't look too closely at his poor, swollen nose.

6

NIKKI TOOK FULL ADVANTAGE of Adam's hotel-room shower, trying to soap and rinse all the "bad-girl" cooties off her body. The problem was that despite the niggling sense of shame she still felt at being scantily clad, popping out of a cake for dozens of men and burning up the sheets with an unknown guy—being bad felt really, really good. Being bad felt excellent, truth to tell. Liberating.

She felt as if she'd spent her entire life until now squeezed into a brutal pair of polyester support hose, and she'd just cut herself free. What a great feeling. She laughed out loud in the shower, and the sound bounced off the tiles.

She now had a delicious secret, like the famously nonexistent Victoria. Nobody ever had to know besides her and Adam. But as her laughter faded, spiraling down the drain with the water sluicing off her body, Nikki hugged herself.

For all that the sex had been spectacular, Adam had never once kissed her or touched her anywhere intimate with his mouth. Translation: he thought that she might have something communicable, like an STD. Translation: he didn't believe that this was the first time she'd danced nearly naked for men. Translation: he thought she was at best loose and at worst some kind of—

She put that thought out of her mind. Adam may have given her three orgasms, but she would probably never see him again.

Well. That was for the best. She was quite sure he wouldn't respect her in the morning. And it was up for debate whether or not she'd respect her*self* then. Though why women were somehow more worthy of blame than men in these situations, she'd never understand.

Oh, who cared? Sex wasn't about respect anyway. It was about tossing panties on the lamp shade and having a good time. So there.

But Nikki scrubbed her privates again, until they practically squeaked. She rinsed off and stepped out of the shower, avoiding her own face in the mirror as she groped for a towel.

Nikki dried herself then wrapped the towel around her head. The terry cloth had aggravated the twin mosquito bites on her butt again, which completed her crazy emotional arc this evening: she'd gone from scared to slutty to horrified to ashamed to laughing-at-herself to orgasmic to euphoric to ashamed, part two, and now back to dorky.

To top it all off, she couldn't stop thinking about how Adam hadn't kissed her. Why she would obsess about that when the sex had been spectacular made no sense. He wasn't her boyfriend, they weren't dating, so there was no intimacy between them. She should be glad that he hadn't put his tongue in her mouth or put his lips all over hers because that was like sharing something more. But she wasn't glad.

Which meant she was just plumb crazy.

Nikki threw on the hotel robe and belted it. She had the weekend to recover and then she'd start her new job as administrative assistant to the dean at the medical school. She'd be covered from head to toe in a professional outfit, and nobody would ever guess that tonight she'd burst, mostly nude, out of a cake for a bunch of howling, wolf-whistling men. Nobody would ever know that she'd gone back to a hotel with one of those men. This embarrassing incident would remain her own sordid little secret.

Thank the good Lord.

Nikki wiped a pathway through the steam on the mirror and stared herself right in the eyes. *I may be fallen, but I* can *get up.* She did her best to get Adam's comb through her wet, curly blond hair. Then she threw back her shoulders and drew herself up to her full height. She'd face Adam like a queen.

ADAM LAY SPRAWLED buck naked in the center of the bed, unable to move despite the call of his medical books and the throbbing of his nose. He knew he should turn his eyes to the texts and return the ice to his nose, but his body ignored his conscience and continued to make like an amoeba dug into the ocean floor.

When the bathroom door flew open and Nikki emerged breasts-first, like a blond battleship in a bath-robe, he did manage to blink, though. "Wow," he said inanely. "You're all clean."

"Yes," she agreed.

She seemed to be waiting for something.

Adam searched his amoeba-brain for what it might be and came up blank. Then it hit him: she was a dancer and she probably wanted a tip. Well, he didn't have much, but—

Then it hit him much harder. Oh, no. She was a dancer whom he'd taken to bed. Easily. Way too easily.

Hooker, man. She's a hooker! *And after handing three hundred dollars to Gib, you have the sum total of forty-three dollars in your pocket, give or take some change. Better yet, after paying tuition a month ago, and your co-payment at the minor emergency center tonight, you have...*

He did the math quickly.

Only fifty-two dollars and ninety-three cents left unused on your debit card.

What were the chances that her rate was—he did more math—under ninety-five dollars and ninety-three cents?

Nada. Nil. Zilch.

She was a babe.

He chewed the corner of his mouth as he wondered exactly how much she charged and how in the hell he was going to come up with it. Then, worse, he wondered if she'd faked all three orgasms.

"Is something wrong?" Nikki inquired.

"No, no. Not at all." Adam wanted to crawl under the bed. His only option was to call Devon, and he really, really didn't want to do that. Not even a little bit. Shit! How had he gotten himself into this situation?

He rubbed the back of his neck and stared at her hopelessly. Could you put a trick on layaway?

No. He'd already taken delivery of it, so to speak.

Could he get on some kind of payment plan with her?

"Well," she said. "This is awkward."

He produced a feeble smile. *Oh, honey. You have no idea.*

"I think I'll, um, go home, now."

"Sure. I'll walk you to your car." He shot off the bed and into his jeans. He fished around on the floor for his shirt and shrugged into it.

"You've got that on backward," she told him.

So he did. Adam found that he didn't care, though. He really wanted to get this awful explanation over with. He sat on the bed again and ducked his head down on the pretext of putting on his boat shoes, which he could have slipped into easily. "Ah, Nikki. I don't, you know—as a student—have much, ah, money." He risked a peek upward.

She'd drawn her eyebrows together. "I know the feeling. Neither do I."

Great. She wasn't going to give him an inch, was she?

"Yeah. Well, the thing is that I may have, ah, misunderstood the situation, here. I don't know what you normally charge—"

She stared at him, clearly perplexed. Then her face cleared. "Oh, I see what you're getting at. Adam, the dance was free. It was me making things up to you for hurting your nose. I told you that."

"Well," he said, feeling his face flame, "that's very generous, but I know I need to, um, take care of you, so could you give me an indication of...?" His voice trailed off. Jesus, Joseph and Mary, *how* did you ask a woman what price her pussy was?

"Take care of me?"

Oh, come on. The girl couldn't possibly be this stupid. He screwed up his courage and tried to make a joke out of it. "You know. For the rest. I mean, maybe you'll give me a discount since I made you pretty happy, too, but what do I owe you for tonight?"

All color drained out of her face, her mouth dropped open and her eyes went stormy.

Adam cringed. *Oh, shit. Is she not— Oh, shit upon shit upon shit.*

"I'm not a whore, you disgusting creep!"

Not a hooker.

Her face flashed ruddy-red now.

Not a hooker, not a hooker, not a hooker. So what do you do now, Captain Brains? Adam's mouth worked, but no sound came out. Probably because he had no words to get himself out of this colossal catastrophe.

"S-sorry," he croaked.

"Yes, you are. You're one sorry excuse for a man!" She whirled around and started for the door like a defensive end bull-rushing the quarterback.

"Wait!" Adam said. "Where are you—"

The door slammed on his verb.

"—going?"

He cursed. Regardless of his personal mortification, he could not let the girl go running around this neighborhood naked under a robe. Burke men made sure that women got home—or to their cars—safely, under any circumstances. His dad and his grandfather—not to mention his uncle—had drummed that into his head well before the age of twelve.

Adam grabbed his thin wallet, her stilettos, skirt, tiny top and microscopic panties, then tore after her. "Nikki! Nikki, stop."

He caught up with her halfway across the parking lot.

"Get away from me," she snapped at him.

As she spoke, a car came flying into the lot and they both had to jump aside.

Nikki huddled into the bathrobe as if she were cold, even in the moist, hot evening air. She kept walking toward where she'd parked her car, under the scarce shelter of a pineapple palm.

"Look, I humbly and sincerely apologize for insulting you. I didn't think you were a hooker at first, but then you seemed to be waiting for something, and it hit me that maybe the something was money, and then I didn't know what to do because I have less than a hundred bucks to my name—"

Nikki raised her arm, keeping it straight, palm out. "Don't talk to me."

He sighed and slipped his wallet into his back pocket. Then he extended his index finger, upon which was hung her lingerie and her high-heeled sandals. "You may want these."

She snatched them without a word, then the skirt and top, and stalked barefoot next to him as he loped along next to her like a jackass. "Why are you still here? *Go away.*"

"I'm walking you to your car."

"Yeah? What a freakin' *gentleman* you are. Turn around and walk straight to hell, buddy."

Adam sighed.

"And for your information, the only reason I was in that stupid cake tonight is that I got laid off from my job and I haven't started my new one yet."

They arrived at her car and she was evidently so angry that once again, she had trouble getting her key into the lock. Adam started to reach around her to help, but she smacked his arm.

O-kay. He let her scratch up her paint.

"Nikki," he said. "I really am sorry. And in the interest of keeping the facts straight, I wouldn't have… you know…if I thought you were a hooker."

"Go tell your lies to someone else." She finally got the door unlocked and wrenched it open.

"I would actually really like your number," he said, even though he knew the request was futile.

She froze and then turned to him with an expression of incredulity. "I *know* you didn't just say that."

Adam shoved his hands into his pockets. "Yeah. I did. And I'm serious." And, inexplicably, he was. Something about her sweetness and her outrage—especially now that he'd gotten his head out of his ass and could see *her* clearly—appealed to him. The fact that she was crazy sexy, and *obviously* was not a stripper—or a hooker—didn't hurt.

She leaned her face close to his. "No, you're *insane.* Not to mention brain-dead. You can't possibly be in school—unless you're studying *fiction.*" She threw herself into the car and slammed the door.

Adam opened and then closed his mouth. He fought the urge to tell her that he was in the top ten percent of his class in medical school, and eventually planned to specialize in oncology.

It was completely alien, this urge, because he spent most of his time deliberately *not* telling women that he was in medical school.

Why? Because, unfortunately, that information tended to create instant dollar signs in their eyes. They didn't understand that after four years of med school, he'd do years of residency for worse pay than a lot of office managers received. And after *that,* he'd start at a lousy base physician's rate, also crippled by close to

a decade of student loans. On top of which was medical malpractice insurance.

But most women didn't have an inkling of any of
this. They stuck to him like glue and began to try to do
his laundry and bake him cookies and weird shit like
that. Then they got resentful when he had no time for
them because he had to study.

So Adam kept his mouth clamped shut and stolidly
accepted Nikki's rage. He supposed he deserved it.

Nikki turned the key and revved the engine.

Gloomily, he wished for Dev's delight and expertise
in the fine art of insults. What would Dev have said to
the fiction comment?

Dev would have leaned in close to her and probably
blown a ring of smelly cigar smoke around her head,
letting it settle like a lasso around that long, sexy neck
of hers. Then, the clever asshole would have come up
with something brilliant and roped her back in like a
baby calf.

"Darlin'," Dev would have drawled, "how right you
are. I'm studying fiction and you're the smart, sassy
heroine of my dreams."

Then, once Nikki had made gagging noises, Dev
would wink and add, "Now, what say you take off your
clothes and give this villain a kiss before I tie you to
those railroad tracks?"

This might provoke a slap, whereupon—Adam had
actually *seen* him do this successfully in a bar—Dev
would commandeer the hand committing the violence,
twirl Nikki into his arms, and smooch her soundly.

Granted, he'd once gotten a stiletto heel stabbed
through his instep after pulling this, but Dev being
Dev, he'd claimed that it was worth it.

Adam was so caught up in the extremely disturbing

image of Dev kissing Nikki—and he, Adam, wanting to punch him in the nose for it—that he failed to notice that her VW Bug was poised to run him right over as he stood in the glare of its headlights.

She rolled down the window. "Move or become a pancake," she growled. "And don't think I'll take you to the E.R. this time, either. I wouldn't even drag you by the back bumper."

Adam decided, especially given the polite nature of her request, to get the hell out of the way.

7

DESPITE HER ANGER, Nikki was dead asleep at 2:17 a.m., when someone started pounding on her door. Someone who didn't care if this was rude and obnoxious. Someone who was, despite Nikki's attempts to ignore the noise, relentless.

She had a bad feeling about who it might be. She crawled out of bed and pulled on a pair of shorts under the oversize Miami Dolphins T-shirt she'd worn to bed. Then wearily, blearily, she stumbled toward the door and put her eye to the peephole. She winced when she saw Yvonne standing outside.

"Nikki, you open this door! I know you're in there because your car's in the parking lot. So open up." Yvonne didn't look happy. In fact, the brassy-red highlights in her black hair seemed to vibrate with rage.

Nikki also noted the dark circles under her neighbor's eyes, the smeared black eyeliner accentuating them, and the rusty-red lip gloss she wore. Her neighbor looked like nothing so much as a zombie ready to sink her teeth into Nikki's flesh.

It seemed a *very* bad idea to open the door to Yvonne of the Dead.

But she started pounding on the painted metal again, and this time added screaming and cursing to her repertoire. The gist of the message, studded with F-bombs galore, was that Nikki had really screwed up and that she was going to answer for it.

"Now open this door!"

Nikki sighed. She was wide-awake anyway, and they might as well get this over with. It wasn't going to be any more pleasant tomorrow or the next day.

She reluctantly unfastened the security chain and slid back the bolt. Within seconds, Yvonne's index finger was stabbing her in the chest.

"Ow—"

"What the *hell* were you doing back there at the bar? You freakin' *coldcock* a guy and then *leave?* Do you know how bad you made me look? *Do* you?"

"I didn't coldcock him. I jumped out of the cake and he was standing sort of behind me, and my elbow slammed into his nose—"

"Spare me the details, *estupida bruta!* Like I care." Yvonne was literally spitting mad. Tiny drops of saliva flew from her mouth and spattered Nikki's face. Ugh.

Nikki removed Yvonne's index finger from her breastbone and went into the kitchen for a paper towel. Undeterred, her neighbor followed her.

"Do you even care that you made me look like a moron?" she asked. "That we had to deal with all the drunk, pissed-off, horny guys who then called the competition, so that we lost the business? Do you care that because of you, I forfeited not only my booking fee, but future gigs with my *own* goddamned *cousin?*"

Nikki wet a paper towel and mopped her face with

it. "Yvonne," she said quietly, "it was an accident. I never meant for any of this to happen. I can't tell you how sorry I am. Really."

"I don't want your lame apology."

"Then what *do* you want?" Nikki asked, stung.

"For starters, I want my money back, the money I loaned you. By the end of the day tomorrow—"

Nikki's stomach did a greasy slide. "But I don't have it yet."

"I don't care. Figure out a way to get it."

"Yvonne—"

"You get it to me by five o'clock tomorrow, or I'm going to take it out of your ass. Understand?"

Nikki was genuinely shocked. "Are you threatening me?"

Yvonne poked her tongue into her cheek and folded her arms under her sizable breasts, which looked like twin torpedoes under her tight white tank top. "Nah, of course not. I'm just tellin' you that come five-fifteen tomorrow and no money, me and Ricky gonna pay you a friendly little visit with some baseball bats we just got autographed by the Marlins."

Nikki shivered as, paradoxically, tiny bullets of sweat broke out at her hairline and under her arms. Ricky was Yvonne's Cro-Magnon boyfriend. He had a protuberant brow and biceps the size of beer steins. He'd also done time for assault and battery on his ex-wife, something that Yvonne insisted was all a big "misunderstanding."

Nikki personally didn't think there was anything to misunderstand about a black eye, a broken jaw and three cracked ribs, but Yvonne maintained that she could take care of herself if Ricky ever lost that lovin' feeling.

Nikki had her doubts, but as Yvonne had pointed out, he had to go to sleep sometime and she was skilled with a serrated-edge knife.

"You understand me, blondie?" Yvonne's voice was every bit as cutting. "You'll be seeing those autographs up close and personal."

A cactus had sprung up in Nikki's throat. She tried to force a couple of words past it, but they got impaled on the spines.

Like an enraged goose, Yvonne angled her nose forward and bobbed her head up and down in rhythm to her next words. "Do. You. Get. What. I'm. Sayin'?"

Nikki nodded.

"Good. Now, besides the money you borrowed from me, you can pay me my booking fee from tonight—fifty bucks—plus another fifty for my trouble."

What? She wanted an extra hundred dollars, too? Nikki opened her mouth to protest, saw the dangerous glint in Yvonne's eye, and closed it again.

"You got something to say? Because I'm being generous. I should charge you for, like, twenty booking fees—"

A thousand dollars. Nikki almost fainted.

"—since that's what I'm going to miss out on, thanks to you, until I can get my cousin to trust me again." Yvonne blew out a malignant breath.

"So, with the extra hundred, that's five hundred bucks."

Blink. Gulp.

"And bring me cash," Yvonne ordered. "Not some rubber check."

Blink. Blink. Nod. Please, just go away and leave me alone.

Yvonne, having vented her rage and asserted her

power, swiveled and marched to the door, each cosmetically enhanced buttock fighting for space in her sprayed-on jeans.

If Nikki hadn't been so tired, demoralized and frightened of the witch, she might have laughed. Instead, she double-locked the door again behind her and slid to the floor. Where was she going to get the four—make that five—hundred dollars she owed Yvonne?

ADAM FIGURED THAT he didn't have the right to be miffed about Nikki denying him her phone number. The night had been one big, humiliating fiasco. No wonder she wanted to forget it—and him. But he wasn't happy.

He was even more unhappy when Dev stumbled through the hotel room door at 4:21 a.m., bringing with him a dense fog of alcohol fumes mixed with the aroma of fast-food burritos. Dev trumpeted his arrival with a burp that reeked of hot sauce and then peed for what seemed like a half hour, without closing the bathroom door. Then he proceeded to snore for the rest of the miserable night.

At 7:09 a.m., he awoke cheerfully despite a raging hangover, popped four ibuprofen and grilled Adam about his evening's entertainment.

"So, dude. Did the hot little stripper grease your pole?"

Adam touched his nose gingerly, lifted his head from the pillow and squinted at him. "Wow, that's such an elegant way of putting things, Dev."

"What can I say? I'm famous for being classy. Well, did she?"

"No. Now go back to sleep."

"You didn't even try to drill her doughnut?"

"Dev, my nose was almost broken."

"Yeah, so? That's at the opposite end of things."

Adam sighed.

"C'mon, just give me a brief rundown. Didja go to the E.R.?"

"Yes."

"Did she find some clothes first, or did she put the docs into cardiac arrest?"

"Yes, she put her clothes on."

"A damn shame. I was afraid you'd say that. So what happened after you left the E.R.?"

"She drove me back here, Dev."

"And? Did she tuck you in? Read you a naked bed-time story?"

"No, Dev. She's actually a nice girl," Adam said stiffly.

"A nice girl," Dev said with a guffaw. *"Right."*

"She is."

After Adam had told him a highly edited version of the story wherein he and Nikki had simply talked, Dev assumed a sportscaster's voice. "So Doctor Burke goes down in flames," he announced.

Then he added, "I don't get why she wouldn't give you her number. You're studying to be a doctor, man. Chicks dig that. You must have done something really crappy for her to stiff you on her phone number."

Studying. Yep. What he should have been doing all night, instead of being a crazed and horny hound, thanks to Nikki. Adam sighed. "I did not do anything crappy." *Liar, liar, dick on fire.*

"Did you have sex with her?"

"That would be none of your business."

Dev grinned unrepentantly. "I know—that's why I'm asking."

Adam made no comment.

"The only reason for a girl not to give you her phone number is that you had bad sex. Lemme guess. You couldn't get it up. Or you blew early. Which was it?"

"I'm not discussing this with you, Dev."

"Why not? It's just biology. Having erectile dysfunction is nothing to be embarrassed about, you know—"

"I do not have E.D.! We did not have bad sex!"

"Aha. But you did have sex."

Adam said nothing.

"So was it good, then?"

I made the girl come three times and she finally begged me to stop. You tell me. But Adam didn't say a word aloud. Another rule of Burke men: gentlemen didn't kiss and tell. "I never said we had sex. All I said was that we didn't have *bad* sex."

"I'm not getting anything out of you, am I?"

"Nope. So how was *your* night, Dev? Did *you* have sex?"

"Not even with myself," he said regretfully. "Too drunk. We did get two alternative strippers after about an hour. They got a little upset when I ripped off my shirt and went onstage to dance with them. One took off, but the other one stayed to party. She was a good sport. The bartender, now—he's another story. Got all riled up because the boys took his whole container of sliced limes and threw them at me."

"Ah. That explains why you smell a little tropical, on top of the b.o.—and the miasma of burrito farts, alcohol and morning breath. I don't suppose you'd consider showering and using some mouthwash?"

Dev shrugged philosophically. "Why would I clean up for *you?*" He yawned. "I'll wait until later. What d'you say we go facedown until five, then shower, spruce up and go find us some cute bridesmaids?"

"Sure, man," Adam said without enthusiasm. None of them could possibly be as hot as Nikki. Too bad he'd never see her again. "Whatever you say."

He couldn't go facedown. He needed to stay face-up and at least semi-vertical, with his books. Suddenly Dev's snoring held more appeal: it would help to keep Adam awake.

He made coffee, poured it into a tall paper cup and dumped every available sugar packet into the vile liquid, stirring it up with a pen. Then he took a giant gulp, burning his mouth, and cracked open a chapter on molecular biology.

Reading was a challenge, since his nose was swollen… and every time he looked down it to focus on the text, he revisited the image of Nikki bursting out of the plywood cake, her elbow smashing into his face because he'd been so stupefied by her delectable ass in the red G-string that he forgot to dodge.

He was focused on biology, all right—every molecule in him wanted to fuse with every molecule in her. Again.

8

NIKKI SAT IN HER LITTLE blue Beetle, clenching her hands on the wheel. She was parked in her mother's driveway, in front of the small two-bedroom stucco house she'd grown up in. In the front yard was the now huge royal palm that she and her mom had planted in a pot as a seedling and carefully tended because the more mature ones cost hundreds of dollars.

The streamlined palm stood straight, proud and true in the late-morning sunlight and seemed to reproach her for being here, for needing to ask her mother for a loan to cover yet another loan. It fed itself through photosynthesis and water, taking nothing that it didn't need and giving back oxygen to the atmosphere in return. Nikki envied it. She might not be the most ambitious person on the planet, but she did want to find a way to give back to others.

Right now, though, she had to focus on *paying* back, not giving back. She hated being in debt.

Slowly she got out of the car, her feet feeling like lead in her old Crocs as she moved up the driveway toward the varnished front door of the tiny home.

Cement-and-resin garden frogs in all shapes and sizes dotted the little porch. Why her mother had a thing for frogs, she didn't know. Maybe she hoped that they would all turn into princes one day?

Nikki averted her eyes from the roof, which had once been an expanse of lovely terra cotta barrel tiles that had now faded and cracked and succumbed to blackish green mildew. The roof was an ongoing nightmare that her mother couldn't afford to fix.

Tara Fine, her mom, had dark red hair that owed its richness to Clairol. She had abundant curves and owed those to her own baking. And she had the same large, seawater-green eyes as Nikki. She wore no wedding ring since she'd never been married—Nikki's dad, the drummer in a band, hadn't offered that option.

She'd raised Nikki by herself with a lot of love, very little money and some occasional babysitting from her sister, Dee, and her parents, Nikki's Gran and Poppy.

Tara opened the door at Nikki's knock and immediately enfolded her in a big, squishy, wonderful hug. Like the palm tree, it made Nikki feel guilty. She wasn't here out of daughterly affection, she was here to ask for money. Money that her mother probably didn't have to spare.

But Aunt Dee had her own issues, so was out as a source of cash, and none of Nikki's friends could loan her five hundred dollars right now.

"Hi, sweetie," Tara exclaimed, smelling of vanilla extract, butter and flour. "What a nice surprise. Good timing, too. I just pulled a tray of raspberry scones out of the oven."

The house smelled wonderful as Nikki stepped inside, like a smaller version of Sweetheart's, her mother's bakery. The living-room walls were painted in a soft cinnamon color, airy olive curtains that Tara had made herself hung in the windows, and the love seat and matching chair were draped in striped-gold-and-olive slipcovers. Instead of throw pillows, there were cats on the furniture. Cats that blinked sleepily, yawned and stretched. Cats in every color: tabby, calico, orange, white and black.

Nikki wrinkled her nose as she caught the familiar ammonia stench that underlay the aroma of the fresh scones. With so many cats inside, it was simply impossible to disguise the presence of their by-products—especially since the dear kitties were partial to the dozens of potted plants and delicate fruit trees that filled the house.

The sunroom, in particular, was in constant disarray, since the cats chewed on the wicker furniture, used the cushions for sharpening their claws and gleefully dug the soil out of the plants, sending it flying, in order to make their deposits. Tara scolded them but it did no good.

Nikki followed her mother through the vanilla-painted dining room, where books and papers constantly covered the table since Tara had started taking classes part-time. Nikki's childhood paintings of lopsided cakes and pies and cookies still hung framed on the walls in this room, though they embarrassed her and she'd begged her mother to take them down.

Tara had painted the kitchen a chocolate-brown with bright white trim. A tiny bistro table and two chairs occupied the nook by the window. Shiny copper bakeware hung in artistic arrangements here, along with framed magazine pictures of fantastic chocolate creations and elaborate gingerbread houses. A solid wall of colorful dessert cookbooks stood opposite the stove. This room, more than any other, defined her mother's life.

"Would you like whipped cream on your scone?" Tara asked.

Nikki chuckled ruefully. "Sure, why not add another couple hundred calories to the four hundred in the scone."

Her mother waved a dismissive hand and got two delicate porcelain plates out of a cupboard. She loved to scour antiques shops for two sets of things like tea cups and saucers, plates and bowls. Then when she threw the occasional party, she'd mix and match them all to the delight of the guests.

"Coffee? Tea?"

"Do you have some leftover coffee from earlier? I'll ice it."

Tara nodded and then cast a shrewd glance in her direction as she plated a couple of the golden-brown scones. "What's wrong, sweetie?"

"Nothing," said Nikki, but she knew she hadn't fooled her mom.

"Hmm. I always walk around with a frown and a wrinkle in my forehead when nothing's wrong, too."

That brought a smile to Nikki's face despite her mood. She mixed her iced coffee and the two sat at the table. One bite of fresh, hot raspberry scone with whipped cream did a lot for her spirits. A moan of pleasure escaped her and she scarfed down the rest of it in record time.

"All right," said Tara. "What's on your mind?"

Ugh. Okay, it was time to 'fess up. "Mom…I hate to ask you this. But could you possibly loan me five hundred dollars until I get my first paycheck in two weeks?"

There was the tiniest, most infinitesimal hesitation before Tara said, "Of course. No problem."

Nikki squirmed. "I wouldn't ask if I weren't kind of desperate."

"I know that. I can count on one hand the number of times you've ever asked me for money. When do you need it?"

"Um. By four-thirty today."

Tara set down her coffee. "Are you in some kind of trouble, honeybun?"

"No, no. Of course not. It's just that I had to borrow the money from someone who, um, unexpectedly needs it back right away."

Her mother looked at the clock on the stove, which said 10:45 a.m. "Well, I was hoping we had more time to chat, but we'd better get to the bank right away. It closes at noon on Saturdays, and I can't get that much money from my ATM card."

Nikki nodded and inspected the crumbs on her plate, feeling terrible. Tara had her classes to pay for, plus the new part-time help at the bakery, not to mention the roof. The last time Nikki had been here when the weather was bad, she'd noticed the old lobster pot sitting on a towel in the hallway, collecting rain from a leak.

"I'll get changed and we can go," her mother said as she stood. Then, unexpectedly, she grabbed for the back of her chair and leaned on it, hard.

"Mom?" Nikki jumped up. "What's wrong?"

Tara blinked and took a deep breath. "Nothing. I got up too fast and lost my balance, that's all."

"Are you dizzy?"

Tara shook her head, but she didn't let go of the chair.

Nikki took her arm, guiding her back into the seat. "Has this ever happened before?" Her mother was only forty-seven—surely too young to be having health issues. Right? But fear coiled low in Nikki's belly.

"N-no."

The hesitation was the giveaway. "Mom, don't lie to me. This *has* happened before, hasn't it?"

"Only a couple of times. It's nothing serious, so don't fuss."

"How do you know it's nothing serious? Have you seen a doctor?"

"Don't be ridiculous. There's nothing to be concerned about."

"You don't really know that, now do you? I'd feel better if you'd see a doctor and get this checked out."

Her mother's mouth flattened mulishly. "You know my opinion of so-called Western medicine. It's a racket. Take this pill, take that pill, have this outrageously expensive test, have that one. Do you know how many people's lives are compromised by the giant pharmaceutical machine? They'd feel a lot better, most of them, if they'd stop taking three-quarters of their prescriptions. They should try acupuncture."

Nikki sighed. "You still haven't gotten health insurance, have you?"

"Oh, that again." Eye roll. "I did look into it, honey, but I simply can't afford those premiums right now. It's a crazy amount of money, just to be able to go to a bunch of arrogant quacks intent on milking the system for every dime they can get. No, thank you."

Tara was more than a little prejudiced against doctors, especially since her sister, Dee, had been disastrously married to one. She'd been what Tara called his "starter wife," the one who'd supported him all through med school, residency and specialization programs. She'd had his children, too, only to be discarded when a hot young sales rep had caught his eye.

"Mom—"

"*Insane,* what they want monthly for a policy." Her mother snorted. "How anyone can afford it is beyond me."

"It has to be less than paying for a major operation on your own, like I'm having to do. And not all doctors are quacks. There are things that acupuncture and herbs can't cure. What if *your* appendix ruptures? What if you find a lump in your breast? What if—"

Tara waved her hand dismissively about this, too, the same as she had about calories. "Nicole, enough. I get it. Okay?"

Nikki ignored her mother's stern tone. "What about the university? Now that you're taking classes, don't you qualify for group insurance on the student plan?"

Tara shook her head. "I'm afraid not. I'm not a full-time student."

"What if you did go full-time?"

"I'd have to sell the business. Unless maybe my daughter wanted to take it over." Her mother shot her a sideways glance.

Take over Sweetheart's? Nikki's heart sank. She liked to bake occasionally, but to do it all day, every day? Never to leave the premises? The thought held little appeal. Sweetheart's was her mother's dream, not hers. The *Forbes* article she'd read in the clinic returned to her mind, along with the concept of a business that benefited single moms.

"Since you don't seem to be jumping at the chance," Tara said dryly, "I think I'll keep my current means of making a living, and do school on the side."

She hadn't thought it possible, but Nikki now felt even worse about borrowing the money from her mother. Still, this wasn't about her—somehow the subject had changed.

"Okay, fine, but you're avoiding the topic. We were discussing the fact that you really need health insurance."

"No, I believe you were. The subject is closed for me. I can't afford it, unless I give up my annual vacation, and I refuse to do that. There's nothing wrong with me that vitamins and exercise can't cure."

"But—"

"No buts." Tara stood again, this time a little warily, but without incident. She exited the kitchen and walked toward her bedroom. "I'm *fine.*"

"Mom, you're gambling with your life," Nikki insisted, following her.

Tara sighed. "Don't be melodramatic."

"You *are.*"

"Well, it's mine to gamble with." Her mother sounded exasperated.

"Maybe so, but there are a lot of people who care about you, and you're gambling with their love for you, too. What you're doing—or not doing—it's…it's…" Nikki searched for a word to express her feelings. "It's *irresponsible.*"

She shouldn't have said it. She knew she'd gone too far as soon as the words were out of her mouth, but her excuse was worry, and this was backed by her own experience in what the lack of health insurance could do to someone financially. It was one thing to struggle to replace a roof. It was quite another to have to sell your whole house to pay off massive debt.

Tara turned on her heel and folded her arms across

her body, her expression closed. "Irresponsible," she repeated.

The worst word in the house. The one Nikki had grasped for unconsciously, instinctively, knowing that it would have impact.

"I'm sor—"

"Yes, well, I specialize in being irresponsible, don't I, Nicole? I got knocked up without being married. Then I decided to have the baby. Worse, I was bull-headed enough to raise her myself instead of giving her up for adoption. I had no prospects, so I started a silly business making cupcakes out of my apartment and to everyone's shock, it took off. My irresponsibility has always served me well. It's paid for your upbringing and your college—"

"I'm sorry. I'm *sorry*, Mom. Please," Nikki said, miserable. "That word shouldn't have come out of my mouth. I'm just— I worry about you. I love you."

Tara's face softened immediately. "I love you, too. Now, let's give this topic a rest and get to the bank before it closes. Okay?"

9

ON MONDAY, NIKKI AWOKE at 5:00 a.m., excited about starting her new job in the dean's office at Palm Peninsula Medical School—even if her mother didn't have much respect for the "quacks" who matriculated.

Being an administrative assistant wasn't her lifelong dream, but she would have money to pay down her debt and she would have medical insurance while she brainstormed a plan for a viable business that helped single moms.

Nikki had worked to forget her weekend misadventures, even if she couldn't quite ban the image of Adam Burke from her mind. Or her body, which had liked him far too much. Thank God she hadn't lost her marbles and given him her phone number.

She'd commanded her spirit to overrule her mind and body when it came to Adam, had paid back Yvonne and on Sunday, had called to check on her mother, making her promise at least to see an acupuncturist if she had another disturbing dizzy spell.

This morning, Nikki started the coffeepot and then stood in her closet, hands on hips, trying to decide which of her two most conservative outfits to wear. One ensemble consisted of a knee-length black skirt and a patterned pastel-pink-and-black sweater. The other possibility involved a knee-length navy skirt and a sailor-inspired blouse with a bow under the wide white collar.

She finally decided on the sailor blouse and navy skirt because they seemed to communicate that yes-sir-right-away-sir image she wanted to cultivate. The blouse also hid the more, er, mountainous terrain of her body.

Nikki showered, dried her hair and pulled it back into a demure knot at the nape of her neck. She applied minimal makeup and no jewelry except for pearl studs at her ears. She debated whether to wear panty hose, but, since nobody in Miami had worn them for at least a decade, decided against them.

Low-heeled navy pumps completed her look, and though she didn't own a navy pocketbook, she had picked up an inexpensive canvas tote striped in red and blue that would hold her things.

Though she took her time, she was ready to go forty minutes before she actually needed to walk out the door, even allowing for traffic delays. This left her with nothing to do but drink an extra cup of coffee, file her nails and be antsy about her first day on the job.

Adam's face insisted on appearing in her mind's eye, so utterly expressionless as she'd refused to give him her phone number. She felt a little bad about that, and she felt worse as her body decided at that very moment to remember how his had felt intertwined with hers.

How his had felt *inside* hers.

Nikki drew the file too sharply across her thumb-nail and broke off the outer corner of it, right down to the cuticle. Great. Just great. Now she'd have to wear a Band-Aid wrapped around it because it looked freakish.

Go away, Adam Burke!

She threw the nail file into her tote, got the bandage and wrapped it around her thumb. Then she took a last swallow of tepid coffee and choked on it when she remembered his fascination with the tiny heart over her privates.

Maybe, just maybe, he'd been disappointed when she'd refused him her number.

Maybe she'd wanted him to try a little harder for it, even beg for it, especially when she'd been so very easy for him. Of course, that easy part reminded her of why she hadn't given him her number. He thought she was a hooker. Despite what she'd said, he thought the worst of her. And that still made her mad.

Maybe by the time she'd threatened to run him over, he'd been convinced she wasn't. Maybe by then he believed her.

But what a stupid word: *maybe.* It wasn't a *yes;* it wasn't a *no;* it wasn't anything definite or useful at all. It was simply something people said when they couldn't make up their minds.

Nikki looked at her watch. Then she tossed the rest of her coffee, brushed her teeth and left for work, still early.

Palm Peninsula Medical School had been founded by a prominent surgeon in the 1920s, and its art-deco architecture reflected that. Even buildings added over the decades had been carefully designed to blend in with the original aesthetic.

Nikki would have a desk in the reception area, close to Dean Trammel. The dean himself had told her during her interview that he'd earned his medical degree from Palm in the early eighties and had gone on to specialize in neuroscience. He'd enjoyed research and teaching more than practice, though, and had made a delighted return to his alma mater a decade before.

He was a mild-mannered gentleman with a full head of salt-and-pepper hair, horn-rimmed glasses and a ruddy complexion.

While Nikki had the slightly uncomfortable feeling that she'd been hired more for her looks and people skills than for her other qualifications, Dean Trammel put her immediately at ease and didn't ogle anything he shouldn't.

"Welcome to Palm Peninsula, Nikki," he said. "You'll be responsible for greeting the public, handling the phone lines and filing. You'll also do some light computer work and make careful documentation when students come to this office with issues. These can range from the admissions process to internships and grant applications, from personal problems to curriculum concerns. Your job is to solve the problem if you can, and channel it to the right assistant here if you can't."

Nikki nodded and smiled.

"If you have any questions while you're getting started over the next few days, feel free to ask Margaret, who's been my right-hand for years."

Margaret, who had been on vacation when Nikki was hired, turned out to be a battle-ax in red lipstick.

The homey touches in her office consisted of one rubber plant and one framed photo of a young Marine. Other than that, the room was utterly sterile and bricked in by light gray file cabinets that loomed over the dark gray carpet.

Margaret had short black hair and small, suspicious eyes. She wore a medium gray suit, a blouse that tied in a bow at her neck, sensible black pumps and dark suntan-colored panty hose.

She stared at Nikki's bare legs with as much disapproval as Nikki concealed while staring at Margaret's hideously veiled ones. Then they both caught themselves, looked up and exchanged twin grimaces.

"How nice to meet you, Margaret." Nikki smiled and extended her hand.

"Welcome," Margaret said in sepulchral tones. She inspected Nikki's manicure, complete with thumb bandage, without removing her own fingers from her keyboard.

Nikki dropped her hand. She noticed that the leaves of the rubber plant all reached for the window, as if trying to escape. The young man in the framed photo stared somberly at her, as if in warning. "What a handsome boy. Is he your son?"

Margaret's sparse eyebrows snapped together. "Nephew. Iraq."

She must worry about him. "Oh, I'm sorry to hear that."

"Why? He's a proud soldier, fighting for his country."

"W-well, yes, of course," Nikki stammered. "I just meant that, um, you must be eager for him to come home."

The black brows beetled further. "I do my job, he does his," Margaret growled.

"Nikki, let me show you the rest of the office," Dean Trammel interjected, to her great relief.

"I'd like that," she said in tones as bright as she could summon. "Margaret, it's been a pleasure."

A sort of grunt was the delightful Maggie Mae's only reply.

"Margaret was overseas when you first came to interview," Dean Trammel said. "But she's been eager to meet you."

If that was eager, Nikki sure didn't want to see reluctant, much less hostile. She produced a polite smile, and was startled to see Trammel wink.

"Margaret is the cornerstone of this building," he said in tones loud enough for the woman to overhear. "We simply couldn't exist without her."

Nikki restrained herself from asking whether they'd paid for the woman to go overseas so that she wouldn't scare away prospective employees.

The dean showed her everything from the copy machine to the kitchenette. Then she followed him into his office and he gave her a stack of files. "This is all correspondence that needs to be typed up, presented for my signature and then sent out. If you have any problems reading my chicken scratch, just ask Margaret." He lowered his voice to a whisper. "Really, she's not so bad once you get to know her. And she'd give a kidney for this place if need be."

Nikki accepted the files and assured Dean Trammel that she wasn't intimidated. But as she turned to go to her desk, she prayed that Mags would never have to give a kidney. Because she'd probably rip it out herself while she kept typing with the other hand and then grouse about why everyone was shrieking.

No job was perfect—that was true. But Nikki wondered how many times per day she'd have to interact with the lovely Margaret. Then she sat down, opened the top file and got to work.

BY THE TIME THE clock's hands had spun to 5:00 p.m.,
Nikki had typed up nine of the dean's letters, answered
and routed twelve phone calls and greeted four students
plus the UPS man. She'd just picked up the stack of
letters with Trammel's approvals and signatures when
the outside door to the reception area opened yet again.
She turned with a pleasant smile to greet the visitor.
When she saw who stood in front of her desk, she
dropped the stack.

"Adam?" she managed to say, in a croak.

"Nikki?" he said, incredulous.

Though his nose was still a bit swollen, he was im-
possibly good-looking even behind those wire-framed
glasses, which only emphasized his broad-chested,
Clark Kent mystique. He broadcast humor and com-
petence, too—as if he could single-handedly save the
world with a stethoscope and a grin, no cape needed.

Moreover, she'd swear that he was using his X-ray
vision to discern that she wore tangerine-colored panties under the navy skirt.

"Wh-what are you doing here?" she blurted, dropping to her knees to pick up the letters. Her hands
shook.

"What are *you* doing here?"

"I work here."

"Well, I go to school here." He smiled as if he loved
the tangerine lace tanga that had now, thanks to her
new position on her knees, pulled snugly against her
in an instant wedgie.

"No, no, no," she said, shaking her head and trying
to tamp down her rising panic. "You don't. You live out
of town. You had a hotel room—you were only here
for a wedding."

"Nikki, all the groomsmen had rooms in the hotel

so that we wouldn't have to drive drunk after partying in Miami."

She cast a glance over her shoulder, but thank God the dean was on the telephone and wasn't paying attention to them. "Adam, listen, you can't say anything about— Oh, God, this is my first day and I really, really need this job—so *please,* please don't tell anyone how we, um, met."

"Okay," he said.

She scrambled to her feet and did a tiny shake of her derriere in an attempt to dislodge the tanga. "I mean it."

"I can see that. I won't say a word."

"Because they'd get the wrong idea, you know, like you did—"

"I didn't get the—"

"You did, um, afterward, and—"

Adam's gaze slid from Nikki's face to somewhere over her shoulder as a gaunt shadow loomed across the desk in front of her. She whirled to find Margaret standing behind her.

"What wrong idea would that be?" Mags asked, her beady eyes fierce and her nose twitching. She scanned Nikki's figure with ferocious disapproval, as if she wanted to wrap it in brown paper and hide it from respectable citizens.

Nikki felt dirtier under her gaze than she'd felt when she'd climbed out of the cake in the G-string and push-up bra in front of all the men. Her tongue dried to the roof of her mouth and all she could do was shake her head and look desperately at Adam.

Fortunately, he was quick on his feet. "Ms. Fine told me she was with the medical school when we met, and I assumed she was a student here, like me."

Mags barely restrained a snort at that ridiculous notion. "And you are?"

Adam introduced himself. "I'm in my second year," he added. "I came by to drop off my application for the Perez scholarship."

Was it Nikki's imagination or had Margaret's face softened as she evaluated him? Did an actual heart beat in her gnarled, petrified chest?

"Well, then," the older woman said. "I know your schedule is grueling, young man." She turned to Nikki, her face hardening again. "Don't keep this poor boy from his studies, Ms. Fine. He doesn't have time for any nonsense."

Nikki felt her face flush. "Oh, no, I—"

"Here, I'll take that. I'm in charge of the Perez apps, hon." Margaret twitched the file folder out of Adam's hands.

Hon? Had she really called him *hon?*

"Is everything here? All your forms and recommendations are complete?" Margaret flipped through the pages.

"Yes, ma'am."

"Excellent. We'll be making the decision by committee in the next two weeks, and then we'll let you know."

"Thank you, ma'am."

"You're welcome." And Mags stood there until Adam left. Then she cast a dismissive glance at Nikki and disappeared as silently as she'd arrived. But her voice carried down the hallway. "Don't think that any of these boys have the time for personal entanglements, Ms. Fine."

Entanglements? As if Nikki were a spider, tripping and then trapping men in her web, for God's sake.

But Mags hadn't finished. "Not to mention that we have a *strict* policy against fraternization with students."

Oh, yes? Well, Nikki herself had a strict policy against hurling staplers at coworkers' heads, but that didn't mean she wasn't tempted.

10

Adam sat in his old Mustang, perspiring in the still formidable evening heat of Miami. He sneezed for the fifth time and cursed whatever chivalrous instinct had driven him to buy a bunch of mixed wildflowers for Nikki, who, of course, hadn't arrived home yet.

His exam had not gone well—he knew that—and yet here he was, not studying again. Wasting time and sweating and losing his focus, all because of Nikki. What was wrong with him?

Had he not learned his lesson in high school?

Evidently not.

He pushed that thought aside. Where did women go after working a nine-to-five job? The grocery store? A yoga class?

Though she'd refused to give him her phone number, he'd remembered her last name from a glimpse at her credit card when she'd tried to pay at the minor emergency center. So he'd used the internet white pages to track down her address and number.

At last his patience was rewarded, and Nikki drove

into the parking lot. She pulled into a spot, got out and then reached into the backseat for some grocery bags.

Her navy skirt pulled tight against her delectable backside, and Adam couldn't help but drink in the view for a moment before he recalled why he was there. He climbed out of the car and approached, floral bouquet in hand.

Adam opened his mouth to greet her suavely but sneezed again instead.

Nikki let out a startled shriek and clocked her head against the Beetle's door frame before whirling around.

"Hi," Adam said, before sneezing again. "Sorry. I brought you some flowers but I think I'm allergic to them."

"What are you doing here?" Nikki asked, rubbing her head with a grimace and looking none too pleased to see him.

"Didn't we have this same conversation earlier today?"

"Yes, but how did you find my address? Frankly, it's a little creepy that you've turned up here."

He winced. "I don't mean to be at all creepy. Just dedicated to trying to apologize."

She just stood there, frowning at him.

"Uh, besides, didn't you say the other night that you had a creep radar? And that it didn't go off around me?"

Her lips twitched, which he took as a hopeful sign. At last she took the flowers from him. "Thank you. They're, uh, beautiful."

The sad truth was that they had once been beautiful, but due to their time with him in the hot car, they now looked a little worse for wear. Their heads hung limply from their stems, and their leaves had lost all vibrancy as the sun and the heat leached and then boiled off their oxygen.

"Not so much," Adam mumbled.

She stared down at the bedraggled flowers, unable to contradict him.

"But you are," he added. "Beautiful, that is."

She tilted her head and evaluated him. "Wow. You're really trying hard to butter me up."

Adam felt his cheeks flaming. "Uh, yeah. Yes, I am. Is that a problem?"

She raised an eyebrow. "Possibly. Though I kind of enjoy watching you grovel—"

"Do you? You're too kind. I guess I deserve that."

"But I was warned today not to fraternize with any students at the medical school."

He raised his eyebrows and grinned. "Well, that's okay, then. Because my instincts toward you are anything but fraternal. And may I point out that we are nowhere near the medical school right now."

"You're bad," she said, shaking a finger at him.

He nodded. "The worst."

"And you should know that I'm only still talking to you because you hold my job in your hands."

"Right. There is that." He hoped she knew he was kidding. He moved closer to her and took some of the grocery bags out of her hands. "How'd you like to invite me in?"

She shook her head. "I don't think so."

"I'll keep groveling if you do. Providing you with sick satisfaction. How can you turn that down?"

She laughed, then bit her lower lip. "I really *was* warned about associating with students."

"And how will they ever know?" He dropped his

voice and looked around mock-surreptitiously. "Do you think you were followed?"

"Of course not," she admitted.

"So…?"

"Well, okay, you can come in for a beer or something—"

He waggled his eyebrows. "Or something."

"Don't push your luck." She took the remaining bags from the car, hitched a striped tote bag over her shoulder, and then mesmerized him again by walking toward the building. He caught a subtle, a very faint, triangular line under that navy skirt. It disappeared between her—

"Are you coming or not?" she called over her shoulder.

He blinked and shuffled his feet forward. "Yes. I mean, I hope to, again. One day."

She glanced at him, clearly understanding his meaning. "How much money did you bring, slick?"

He sighed. "Are we ever going to be able to move past that?"

"Depends," she said, jingling her keys.

"On?"

"Whether I decide to let you off the hook."

"I was afraid it might work that way." He changed the subject. "So who's that undead woman in your office?"

Nikki wrinkled her nose and drew out the syllables as if naming a hemorrhoid cream. "Margaret."

"She doesn't seem to care for you much."

"I think Margaret cares for me about as much as she'd care for a dung beetle that crossed the toe of her shoe. And it's only taken her one day to develop that much affection, too."

"Impressive. I'm tempted to bring her flowers, too, since she seems instrumental in handing out the Perez scholarship."

The words produced a withering glance from Nikki. "What's involved in that?"

"Oh, the Perez foundation only funds an entire year of med school at Palm Peninsula. It goes to a deserving, upstanding, outstanding student who needs the money."

"Wow. A whole year. Maybe you *should* bring Mags some flowers," Nikki said. "No joke."

They began to climb the stairs to the second level, where her apartment was. "But she doesn't have nearly as nice a body—or personality—as you do," Adam said. "And besides, I'd rather get by on my own merits, not calculated flattery or bribes."

"You have merits?" Nikki teased.

"A couple. Well hidden, of course."

She opened the door to her apartment and motioned him inside. "What are they?"

"Let's see…I volunteer with the Alzheimer's patients over at Jackson Memorial. I tutor at-risk kids in math and science. I haven't flunked out of med school yet. And I even do apologies."

Nikki followed him and closed the door behind her. She flicked on some lights.

Her apartment was decorated mostly in yellows and blues. Dark blue couch, soft yellow walls, blue-checked kitchen curtains. Nothing was expensive, but it was neat and cheerful.

A small TV perched in an oak entertainment unit opposite the couch. A few books kept company with some framed photographs and knickknacks.

Adam picked up one of them after taking the grocery bags into the kitchen. "Is this your mom? Your home?"

Nikki nodded, chewed at her lip again and sighed.

"What's wrong?"

"Nothing."

He made a gesture for her to continue talking.

"Her house needs a new roof," Nikki finally said. "And she has no way to pay for it."

"That's tough. I'm sorry."

She shrugged and changed topics. "So you're a medical student."

Adam shoved his hands into his pockets. "Yeah." He waited for that I'm-so-impressed look, but it never came. Interesting. Neither did the glazed-over, dollar-signs-in-the-eyes expression. If anything, she seemed disapproving.

She shook her head. "When I turned around and saw you standing there, I almost peed in my pants."

Adam cleared his throat and pushed up his glasses. "It's always been a dream of mine to affect a woman that way," he said dryly.

"Oh, you know what I mean. I was petrified."

"You weren't even a little bit happy to see me again?" He moved toward her.

"No." But the corner of her mouth quivered. She moved to the refrigerator, opened it and reached in for a beer. "You were my worst nightmare."

Adam moved closer, so that when she emerged she turned and faced the wall of his chest.

"Oh…" She extended the beer bottle.

He took it, wrapping his fingers partly around hers so that they held it together. "So. Are you a little bit happy to see me now?"

A pulse beat double-time at the left side of her throat. She swallowed.

"Hmm?" Adam reached out and tucked a curly, golden strand of hair behind her ear. He stared at her perfect, lush mouth with its voluptuous bottom lip.

She nodded and swallowed again.

He took a step closer, and to his disappointment, she dodged out from between him and the refrigerator while he tried not to remember what she looked like naked—and failed miserably. He stood in a state of semi-arousal and took pulls on his beer as she bustled around the tiny kitchen, putting his flowers into water and arranging a plate of cheese and crackers.

"Have a seat," she told him, gesturing toward the couch.

So he did.

Nikki followed him and set down the plate. Several cubes of cheese, a pile of crackers and a few olives winked up at him, a poor substitute for what he really wanted. He started to envy the randy little pimentos inside the cushy flesh of the olives. Damn it. That was truly pathetic.

"Help yourself," Nikki prompted him, and he watched the way her lips caressed the wineglass as she drank.

Yeah, he'd like to help himself, all right. He shot her a peremptory smile and snatched one of the evil, sexually mocking olives. He popped it into his mouth, savaged it and swallowed. Then he poured beer after it, the oral equivalent of a cold shower.

He should be studying. He knew that. He shouldn't even be here. But…he was. He'd been unable to stay away.

"Adam, why are you here?" Nikki asked. "Did you come for sex?"

"What kind of a question is that to ask?" Adam tugged at his collar and shifted once again on the couch.

"Did you?"

He squinted at her. "Are you asking me," he said slowly, "if I came over to take advantage of the situation? Sex for silence? Is that the kind of person you think I am?" He heard the rising anger in his tone. "Really, Nikki?"

His outrage seemed to reassure her. "No, I didn't really think that. But I guess I needed to be sure."

"I came because you were obviously upset to see me in the dean's office, and I wanted to let you know that you have nothing to worry about."

"And the flowers?"

"I brought those because I wanted to make you feel better about the whole weekend."

She took another sip of wine, her green eyes evaluating his face over the rim of the glass.

He felt that she was still waiting for him to say something, but he wasn't sure exactly what. "I like you, Nikki. I really like you. I want a do-over. Will you consider it?"

11

SOMEHOW, ADAM HAD MANAGED to say the right thing, because Nikki softened up and came to sit with him on the couch, instead of staying in the chair opposite. And after a couple of glasses of wine, a good laugh and a tickling session that devolved into stroking and petting, she got downright friendly.

After friendly, to his disbelief, came naked. Somewhere in the recesses of his primitive brain he learned a useful lesson: *good things come to men who apologize.*

The couch should have blushed, as Adam buried himself repeatedly in Nikki's body, but it was only a piece of furniture, after all. He'd never really imagined that she'd let him make love to her again so soon, but she seemed as insatiable for him as he was for her.

"Oh, yes…yes! Just like that. Oh, Adam…"

His gaze swept the coffee table and those smug little olives no longer had the power to mock him. He no longer felt like an exhausted medical student, but like the king of the universe, king of the sex gods, king of Nikki, who was panting wildly and moaning beneath him.

The demure office worker had become his own personal X-rated dream girl.

He leaned forward and took her breasts into his palms, changed his angle, slid deeper. His eyes had begun to roll back and Nikki made a low, keening sound that signaled an imminent loss of control, when his cell phone split the air.

Startled, he slipped out of her for a moment while it continued to ring, and she made a noise of feminine frustration as he repositioned himself. But now a ding signaled a text message. It was followed by another ding.

He stole a quick peek at the small window on the phone.

Test a.m.! Where R U?

Shit. He was supposed to be at his study group meeting. They had another test in Foundations of Medicine in the morning, and here he was making like a billy goat. Was he crazy? Losing his discipline again? The specter of falling back into Loserville reared its ugly head.

"Adam?"

Without realizing it, he'd stopped and slipped out again.

A naked Nikki eyed him in disbelief. "Are you *looking at your cell phone?*"

"No! No, of course not."

But it was too late.

Nikki snapped upright like a switchblade once the button is pushed. Full of righteous rage, she looked as lethal as a knife, too. Her eyes glittered dangerously.

"Uh, I can explain," he said.

She shook her head slowly back and forth, looking like a hot, blonde, naked bull pawing the earth.

With him frozen in front of her, the inept toreador.

"You don't understand," he said desperately.

She didn't charge. She grabbed the cell phone and threw it at his head.

He ducked and dove for his jeans, but she stepped on them and then reached for his unfinished beer. Evidently, hell had no fury like a woman forced to share attention with a cell phone.

Nikki upended the beer as he gave up on the pants and crawled for his shirt, so instead of splashing over his head it ran down his butt crack, then foamed and fizzled over his protesting yarbles.

With a hiss of disgust, Adam leaped over the couch and flattened himself against the back of it. "Nikki, I'm sorry! I forgot that I'm supposed to be somewhere right now—"

"I should have known better than even to *think* about dating a med student!"

"What's that supposed to mean?"

Nikki growled something incomprehensible about assholes, starter wives and pagers. Then she pelted his head with cheese cubes.

"Aw, no, no, no—"

Followed by crackers.

"I *said* I'm sorry!"

And olives, which packed a surprising little wallop when they hit a man square in the temple.

"Shit, are you a back-up pitcher for the Marlins?"

"Captain," said Nikki wrathfully, "of my high-school softball team."

The plate caught him in the kidneys as he ran for the door. "Ouch!"

"Champion Frisbee player, too."

He wrenched at the doorknob. "Anything else I should know?"

"Yes," she said succinctly. "Now you will never, ever taste my homemade cheesecake."

Aw, man. He loved cheesecake. "What flavor?" He pulled the door open.

"I make every flavor. I grew up in my mom's bakery."

"You can cook?"

"Can a fish swim?"

His stomach growled. "Nikki, can't we talk this through?"

"No. Get. Out."

"Can I at least have my clothes?"

She stalked to where he'd left them on the carpet, gathered them up and threw those at him, too.

He clutched them to his privates and crab-walked out.

Then she kicked the door shut in his face, leaving him with her naked image seared forever in his brain.

Adam stood there and wondered how things had gone from so good to catastrophic within thirty seconds. Man had enough problems without the introduction of technology into his miserable life.

Expensive technology. Technology with notes and contact info and downloaded articles from the internet. Oh, hell.

He thought about knocking on the door to ask for his cell phone, but figured his chances of survival if he did so were nil to none.

A jingle of keys a couple of doors down had him quickly glancing to the left.

"Well, hello," Nikki's neighbor said. She had long

black hair, a steely edge and wore too much makeup. She also looked vaguely familiar.

He shot her a sickly grin.

"Hey, Naked Dude. Don't I know you?"

"Nope." But she did look familiar.

She laughed, in a nasty sort of way.

He suddenly remembered where he'd seen her before: she'd wheeled in the cake at Mark's bachelor party. But he was not having this conversation. And the sound of footsteps hitting metal indicated that someone else was coming up the stairs.

Adam turned so that at least Nikki's neighbor wouldn't get the full monty, and jumped into his pants.

"Nice buns," she said.

He reddened, feeling like a piece of meat.

"You need a part-time job, honey? Because I got some bachelorette parties coming up. And none of the girls'd complain if *you* came jumping outta the cake."

Adam shot her a speaking glance, and stuffed his boxers into his pocket. Then he shrugged into his shirt and turned away, only to collide with the guy coming up the stairs.

"Ay! Watch out where you goin', *pendejo.*"

Adam muttered an apology, scooped up his shoes, and fled.

NIKKI PICKED UP the cheese cubes first, then the crackers and finally the olives. She was simply too angry and mortified to cry. Each little thunk expressed her rage as she lobbed the offending morsels into her kitchen waste can.

Bas—thunk—*tard!* Thunk.

Then she had to get down on her hands and knees with a wet dishrag to scrub the beer out of her rug.

This required a whole different rhythm of fury, and she imagined, with twisted pleasure, that the rag was sandpaper and the rug was Mr. Jerk's face.

How *dare* he look at his phone while they were—

What kind of person did something like that?

And while he'd done intimate, highly erotic things to her, he *still* had never once kissed her on the lips. That was just weird. And wrong. And insulting.

Not that she'd ever, ever, give him the chance to come near her lips again at this point. There were some things that a girl could not forgive. And rubbernecking at a cell phone during hot sex was definitely one of those things.

She tossed the beer-soaked rag into her kitchen sink and stalked off to get her fluffy yellow terry robe with Tweetie Bird embroidered on the pocket.

Then she stalked back into the kitchen and pulled out eggs, cream cheese and butter. She left them on the stovetop to warm to room temperature.

She settled onto her much-abused sofa, the scene of the crime, and switched on the television. Half a bad sitcom later, Nikki meandered toward the bathroom and encountered Adam's cell phone with her toe. She glared at it and fantasized about tossing it down the garbage disposal.

But instead, she indulged her natural female curiosity—no, it was *not* nosiness—and looked at the screen.

Test a.m.! Where R U?

Hmm. Adam had said he was supposed to be somewhere. Studying, by the looks of this.

He was a medical student. They did spend twenty

of every twenty-four hours studying. And the guy had taken time to drive over to her apartment with flowers…

No. She was not cutting him any slack. *He had looked at his cell phone in the act!*

But. It wasn't as if he'd dialed the thing, after all. It had rung. Then chirped. And then chirped again.

She'd been distracted by it, too.

As if programmed by the devil, the cursed thing rang again, in her hands. She almost dropped it.

Instead, she pressed Talk.

"Burke, where are you and your notes? We've been here almost an hour. Do you want us all to fail? What the hell, man?"

Nikki chewed her lip.

"Hel-*lo?* Adam?"

"He's not available right now," she said.

"Who is this?"

"But he's on his way." And she clicked End Call, ignoring the masculine squawk on the other end of the line.

Nikki had a mental tussle with herself as she washed her hands, then melted butter for her signature homemade graham cracker crust. She had every right to be angry. And she was.

Was this how things had been every day in Aunt Dee's marriage? Probably.

With the back of a large, smooth spoon, she pressed the graham-cracker mixture flat into the bottom of her cheesecake pan. Adam's cell phone rang again, but she ignored it.

She wasn't his secretary. She wasn't even his girlfriend, or, God forbid, his starter-wife-in-training.

She whipped the cream cheese with sugar, added

the eggs one at a time, and then stirred in vanilla, fresh sliced peaches and a tablespoon or two of peach schnapps.

Then she poured the mixture over the crust and slid it into the preheated oven.

Adam's cell phone rang again, and she sighed.

She let it ring again before she answered. "Hello?"

"Nikki?" Adam said tentatively.

"No, it's the Jolly Green Giant."

"I, uh— I'm really sorry. I didn't mean—"

"If you want your phone back," she said, "you can come by the office tomorrow. Call first. I'll have Margaret give it to you."

A small silence ensued. "Okay," Adam said, sounding defeated. "I guess there's nothing else I can—"

She shook her head, but of course he couldn't see her.

"Okay," he said again. "Thanks. Goodbye."

"Yeah. Bye."

12

NIKKI WORE TWO industrial-strength sports bras under her pink-and-black sweater the next day, and noted with satisfaction that they flattened her by at least two cup sizes. Unfortunately they were also hot, but that couldn't be helped. She was not going to lose this job because her boss couldn't help ogling two stupid bumps on her chest.

Not that the dean had said or done anything inappropriate, but she'd found herself in uncomfortable situations in the past, and one could never be too careful. And she suspected part of Margaret's resentment of her stemmed from her looks.

Nikki further diminished any residual sex appeal by wearing a pair of flat ballerina slippers instead of heels with her skirt. And once again, she tied her hair into a knot at the nape of her neck. If she had to, she'd even find some clear glasses. Whatever she had to do, she was going to stay employed and pay down her debt.

She would not risk a repeat of what had happened at her last office job—borderline sexual harassment by an older man who then used a flimsy excuse to get rid of her when she made it clear she wasn't interested.

Nikki entered the office with a smile and the peaches-and-cream cheesecake she'd made the night before.

Dean Trammel brightened when he saw it. "What's that?"

Margaret's evil-looking brows snapped together as she growled the same question. "What's *that*?"

"This is one of my signature cheesecakes," Nikki said. "I thought it might be nice with some coffee, for breakfast."

The dean rubbed his hands together. "Yum. I sure will have a piece."

Margaret muttered something under her breath about brownnosers and stomped off to cranky-pants headquarters.

Nikki ignored her, went to the kitchenette and cut everyone a slice—there were two other assistants and an intern, all of whom seemed in danger of losing consciousness after the first bite. Moans of pleasure eddied out from every corner. Nikki enjoyed her coworkers' reactions. She liked baking for friends every so often— she simply couldn't picture herself doing it full-time, like her mother.

Dean Trammel wiped his mouth with a napkin and took a sip of coffee. "You made this?"

She nodded.

"Are we voting Nikki a raise, everyone?" he joked.

"Hear, hear!"

Nikki felt heat rising to her cheeks. "I'm glad you like it," she said. "I'm going to take a piece to Margaret."

Everyone exchanged uncomfortable glances and

made excuses to leave the kitchen, toting their cheese-cake and coffee with them.

Nikki raised her chin, squared her shoulders and picked up the plate. Then she marched it into Marga-ret's office. "Hi," she said. "I thought you might like a piece of this."

Margaret bared her teeth. It looked like she wanted a piece of something, all right: a piece of Nikki's dead carcass. "I don't eat sweets."

"Oh, just one bite can't hurt, can it?" Nikki set the plate down on her desk, along with a fork and a napkin.

Margaret eyed the slice of cheesecake as if it were an old, stinky shoe. But in the face of Nikki's pleasant, persistent smile, she sawed off a piece of it with the side of the fork and brought it up to her lips, her eyes narrowed.

Nikki resisted the urge to say, "Choo-choo!"

Margaret shoveled in the bite between her dry, scar-let lips. She chewed. And her eyes widened. An expres-sion of exultation tried its best to dawn across her face before she slapped it back into the murky depths of her soul to cower again in the sludge.

"Cheesecake," she said, "is fattening."

Nikki shrugged. "Maybe a little bit."

Margaret glowered at her and pushed the plate away until it teetered at the edge of her desk. Did she expect Nikki to bus it back to the kitchenette? If so, she'd be disappointed.

"Um, listen, Margaret. That boy who brought you the Perez scholarship application yesterday? Adam Burke? Well, he left his phone by accident. Can I leave it in your care so that he can pick it up later?"

"Why can't he get it from you?"

"Oh. Well. I took your warning about not fraternizing with students a bit seriously, then, didn't I?" Nikki dropped the phone on her blotter. "Silly me." With a little wave, she turned and left Mags's office, making her way back to her own desk.

It was just a tiny bit gratifying to hear the clink of a fork on china as soon as she was out of sight. Ha!

ADAM USED A FELLOW STUDENT'S phone to call the dean's office before going over there, as Nikki had instructed him to do. Her voice when she answered was cool and professional; she gave no hint of anger—which made him feel almost worse than if she had.

There was no sign of her when he walked in, though she'd been sitting at the reception desk the day before. She was probably at lunch.

So he knocked on the partially open door behind the desk, and Margaret, the undead woman, looked up from her computer. "Hi," he said. "I'm Adam Burke. I came to get my cell phone."

He tried not to stare, but Margaret-the-undead had a white smear across her upper lip, with what looked like graham cracker crumbs stuck to it.

Completely oblivious of this, she smiled and motioned him to follow her.

He did.

"I looked over your essay for the scholarship," she said. "It's excellent." A crumb fell onto the face of his phone as she handed it over to him, but she didn't seem to notice.

"Thank you, ma'am," he said.

"And your track record of volunteer work is very impressive."

"Er, thanks."

"Would you like some cheesecake, young man? I just baked one yesterday."

"I'd never turn down a slice of cheesecake, ma'am. What kind is it?"

"Peaches and cream. My specialty." And she led him into the kitchenette of the place, where sure enough, a third of a cake sat on a platter. "Shh, but I've had two slices already," she told him. "I'd be grateful if you'd take the rest off my hands."

"Um, sure…" Starving medical school students didn't turn down food. Especially not homemade food.

She lifted the entire slab of cake, plate and all, and nested it into some aluminum foil. Then she folded that up into a neat package, gave him a plastic fork, and herded him toward the door.

"Thank you very much," Adam said. "This is so nice of you."

"Don't mention it," Margaret said.

He almost told her about the smear and crumbs on her lip, but couldn't quite bring himself to do it. She might take it the wrong way. She'd see it herself soon enough.

"I'll show myself out," he said.

"All righty, then. You remind me a little of my nephew. I'll keep my fingers crossed for you on the scholarship."

"You're too kind, ma'am." As she turned and went back down the hallway, looking pleased, he exited into the reception area, only to run into Nikki.

Like the day before, she was all business: hair in a bun, loose sweater, flat shoes.

She was still beautiful, but she certainly didn't look like the tousled sex goddess he'd had spread-eagle on the couch the night before.

"Uh, hi," he said, feeling a flush climb his cheeks at the memory of how they'd parted.

"Hi." She frowned. "What's in the foil?"

"Oh. That lady Margaret baked a cheesecake last night and she gave me the rest of it."

"She *what?*" Nikki came out of her chair, clearly outraged.

Why, he didn't know. It wasn't as if it were *her* cheesecake, after all.

"Give me that!" she said, rising to her feet.

"Huh?"

"Give me that cheesecake."

"No," Adam said. "It's mine. She gave it to *me.*"

"She *can't* give it to you—"

"She made it, she can, and she did." He strode to the door. "Jesus, woman. You may be hot, but you're a little unbalanced."

Nikki's cheeks flushed with anger and her eyes got stormy.

Was this rabid PMS? Adam stared at her. "What's your problem? You're not the only one on the planet who can make a cheesecake. And since you've made it clear that I'll never get one of yours, I'm darn well taking this one." With that, Adam got to slam a door in *her* face, thank you very much. It felt good.

But the cheesecake, which he wolfed down on the way to his next class, was even better.

NIKKI REALIZED, as the remainder of her cake sailed out the door with that cell-phone-fixated jerk, that she hadn't gotten one slice of it herself. She'd been too busy serving everyone else.

Fuming, she forced herself to get back to work, typing letters and filing miscellaneous paperwork. She'd made that cake with her own hands, and not only had Margaret taken credit for it, but she'd given the rest of it away. How could she have done it? Margaret was evil. Downright rotten to the core.

What a sad, bitter, venomous sack of estrogen she was. Nikki tried to let her anger go, tried to tell herself that the poor woman had nobody else upon whom to take out her life's frustrations.

She told herself to be the bigger person. And when she went to get another cup of coffee and saw Margaret with the white smear and crumbs across her upper lip, she tried not to be entertained. It was sort of awful, really, to witness the fact that nobody, not one person out of the entire office, had told the woman she needed to clean herself up.

It was more awful, she had to admit, than that butt-headed Adam Burke running off to stuff his face with her cheesecake after treating her the way he had.

Mags's eyes slid away from hers as Nikki glowered at her. The woman stared fixedly at her computer screen and her fingers galloped ever faster across the keys.

Nikki went into the kitchen and got a napkin. She glided with it into Margaret's office and extended it to her. Then she tapped her own lip significantly, turned and left without saying a word—though she was sure that her good deed would not go unpunished.

13

THE CHEESECAKE HAD ALMOST sent Adam into orbit with his backpack full of books, but the score on his Foundations of Medicine test brought him back to earth with a bone-rattling thud.

The number seven was not at all lucky when paired with another seven and staring up at him from a one-hundred-point exam. A seventy-seven was unacceptable and unpardonable.

Dr. Antonio da Silva, the instructor, looked at him with concern in his dark, hooded eyes. *"Como estas,"* he asked. "Is everything all right, Adam?"

Mortified, Adam nodded silently.

This was what came of bachelor parties and self-indulgence with girls. He had no time for such things. He had no time for friendships outside med school, much less relationships with women. So it was a damn good thing that Nikki was unbalanced and angry with him.

Because he didn't seem to have the power to say no to her. When he looked at that face of hers, that body... he forgot all about classes like Brain and Behavior. He forgot about *Grey's Anatomy.* He just wanted to get to know *her* anatomy. Up close and personal.

He blinked the images away and stared again at the seventy-seven on top of his exam. There were vague mutterings of unhappiness from the rest of his study group, and they weren't sparing with the dirty looks, either.

Once per week, it was each of their turns to type up and synthesize the notes from this class's lectures and readings, and he'd let them down. They probably weren't happy with their scores, either. He'd have to find a way to make it up to them.

Adam sat numb through the rest of the lecture, trying to focus but internally calculating what grades he needed to achieve for the rest of the semester to wipe out the awful seventy-seven. He'd be okay, but he couldn't afford another slipup like this one. And the Perez scholarship only added to the pressure.

A year's tuition would make a *huge* dent in the crushing student loans Adam would graduate with. People tended to think that upon graduation from med school, guys like him walked into instant practice and made half a million a year.

If only that were true. Instead he would slave away as a resident for under 50k for three years first. Then he might take a modest step up from there. But unless and until he took on a lucrative specialty, he wouldn't make much money—especially since he'd be paying staggering amounts in malpractice insurance premiums.

The seventy-seven screamed, "Loser! Loser!" at him, without mercy. "Backslider!"

He was furious with himself. It wasn't a matter of innate competitiveness or wanting the status of graduating at the top of his class. His grade-point average was crucial to getting into the best specialty programs for oncology later on.

Adam wanted to learn from the top professionals in the country, and those doctors wouldn't bother with a slacker, a guy who couldn't even master the basics. His whole future was at stake—and this time he was on his second chance. He didn't kid himself that he'd get a third.

He looked down at the awful number on the test again and felt not only that he'd let himself down, but had dishonored the memory of his grandfather.

He shoved the test deep into his backpack, his undergrad college ring clinking against the now-clean plate from the cheesecake—he'd washed it in the men's room.

His morale sank even lower as he realized that he had to schlep the damn plate to the dean's office, preferably while beautiful psycho-Nikki wasn't there. He didn't kid himself that Margaret had given him the plate.

Though the sound on his errant cell phone was turned off for class, he felt it vibrate in his pocket. Adam ignored it. The last thing he needed was to have a chat with someone in the middle of da Silva's lecture.

Moments later, a muted ding signified that someone had sent an email. It was followed by four others. *What?* Who needed to reach him this badly?

Adam eased the phone out of his pocket and peered at it, holding it carefully out of sight and under the desk that he sat at. His eyes widened, threatening to fall out of their sockets.

Dev had sent pictures.

Pictures from the bachelor party.

And what pictures they were…

Nikki, exploding out of the cake. Nikki, bending over him, her breasts hanging only inches from his face. A close-up of his face, fixated on those breasts.

Then a close-up of Nikki's backside as she straddled him to inspect his nose. A close-up of the, er, underside of that same backside, G-string disappearing into her…ahem.

The last photo was a full-body shot of her walking him out the door, her arm around him while he held ice to his nose.

Adam closed his eyes. He didn't want to look at these, and Dev needed to lose them immediately. They weren't in the least bit funny. He deleted every picture and started to email Dev back to tell him to do the same, but looked up to see Dr. da Silva frowning at him. Shit.

Adam slid the phone into his pocket and forced himself to concentrate. Most of the time, if ignored, Dev would find someone else to annoy.

THE NEXT MORNING, Nikki was working her way through a stack of filing when the door to the dean's office opened to reveal Adam, sheepishly holding her clean cake plate.

"Hi," he said, squinting at her suspiciously, as if he expected her to lob her keyboard at him.

"Hello," she said coolly. "Did you enjoy the cake?"

He patted his stomach and rolled his eyes upward to indicate total euphoria. "Oh, *maaan.* That was the best cheesecake I've ever had. I do need to give Margaret back her plate, though." He held it up.

Margaret's door was firmly closed.

"It's my plate," Nikki said evenly. "And I made the cake."

He eyed her dubiously. Clearly, he thought she was lying. "Whatever you say, Nikki." But he placed the platter on her desk.

"Why do you think I was so mad that you got it?" she reasoned. "Why do you think I said that Mags *couldn't* give it to you? It wasn't hers to give."

He shrugged, still looking unconvinced.

It *did* sound a little nuts to imply that someone had done what Margaret had done. It wasn't normal. But then, with each year that passed for Nikki, she learned more about the strange psychoses of the human race.

She sighed and dug a card out of her purse. "Here you go. This is my mom's bakery. She makes the exact same cake—that's how I learned to make it. Give it a try and you'll see."

Adam took the card. "Thanks." He shifted from foot to foot like a kid in the principal's office. "Look...I really do want to apologize, again, for the other night."

She held up a hand, palm out, and shook her head.

"No, listen to me. Please." Adam cleared his throat. "We had a test yesterday morning. A tough one. I was supposed to supply the notes for my study group. But because of, you know, the whole weekend, I didn't get them together. And the phone the other night— Well, that was them. My study group. I was horrified that I'd forgotten about the notes, about the meeting, about *everything.* So—not that it makes it any better, really— that's what happened. It wasn't that I was, uh, taking a call from another woman or something."

His eyes behind the wire-rimmed glasses were intense and guileless. She believed him.

"*Is* there another woman?"

"No."

Really? Truly? No other women, for a guy *that* hot?

"So," he continued, "I'm sorry. I really am."

"It's okay," she said, surprising herself. "And I probably shouldn't have, uh, reacted the way I did."

His lips twitched. "The beer down my crack was a bit much."

"You should have seen me trying to get it out of the carpet." But the corners of her mouth tugged up in response to him.

"So did the exam go okay?" she asked.

"No," he said gloomily. "I got a C on it, and nobody in my group seems to be speaking to me, so I don't think they did well, either."

She felt a surge of pity. "I'm sorry."

"I can't believe I forgot—"

"Why do you think you did?"

Adam looked startled, then embarrassed. Red spread across his chest where his shirt revealed the skin, then crept up his neck and suffused his face.

"Why?" He rubbed at the back of his neck. "Well, because I was thinking about you."

It was her turn to blush. "Really?"

"No. I always buy flowers for girls I'm not thinking about."

"Well, what do you think about me now? After the beer down the butt crack and all?"

"I think that the next time we see each other," he said seriously, "I should leave my cell phone in the car."

Nikki laughed, and found that once she started, she could not stop. He joined her.

No doubt irritated by the noise, Margaret opened the door to the reception area and stuck her bony nose out.

"Oh," said Nikki, doing her best to be sober but failing miserably. "Adam came by to give you back your cake plate. He says you make the best cheesecake he's ever tasted."

"Yes, ma'am, you do." Adam said it with a perfectly straight face, as he picked up the platter and handed it to Margaret. Of course, he may not have made up his mind on whom to believe.

"Why...thank you." Margaret's mouth worked and she carefully avoided looking at Nikki. "I'm glad you enjoyed it, young man." A vein at her temple throbbed. She snatched the plate and backed out again, closing the door behind her.

Adam raised an eyebrow.

Nikki raised one right back at him. "I can recite the recipe by heart," she said. "Ingredients—twenty-four ounces of softened cream cheese, four eggs, one egg yolk, three-quarters of a cup of sugar—"

"Wait," he said. "How do you get only the yolk out of an egg?"

"Magic."

"No, really."

"Ancient Chinese secret." She grinned at him.

"Yeah? I saw a book once with some ancient Chinese secrets in it. Those people got into some amazingly contorted sexual positions—" he stopped at the look on Nikki's face "—which of course I would *never* ask you to try," he finished lamely.

"No, of course not," she agreed. She kept a smile on her face as she spoke her next words, to soften them a little bit. "Because despite the fact that you're hot, I'm not interested in being a booty call when you have an occasional spare half hour, okay? Sorry."

14

Adam stared at her, nonplussed. He rubbed at the back of his neck again. Hell, was he blushing for the tenth time today?

"*What?* I never meant— That is to say, you're *not.* I don't think of you that way."

Nikki looked down at her desk, then up at him again without responding.

"I want to take you out on a real date sometime. You know, dinner and a show." As soon as the words were out of his mouth, Adam could have shot himself. Where was he going to get the money to take her out to a nice place? And more important, where was he going to get the time? Wasn't the C on his test warning enough to stay away from her?

He shoved that thought out of his mind. The money he could borrow from Dev, but the time he'd have to steal from other days. If he studied one hour later from Monday through Thursday, maybe he could justify a four-hour date on Friday.

"Does it give you a stomachache to ask a girl to dinner?" Nikki asked.

"Huh?"

"You just got this pained expression on your face."

"I did? No. Of course not. I was thinking of…of a paper that I have due."

She shook her head.

"So how about it?" he asked. "A date."

"Frankly, if you're thinking about a paper even while you're asking me, then it's not a great idea, Adam. And you know I'm not supposed to fraternize with students."

"Oh, come on, Nikki. Give me another shot."

"Look, Adam," she said, lowering her voice. "I need my job and we shouldn't even be talking about this here. Margaret is only a few steps away behind a thin door. Yes, she's on the phone, so she can't hear us, but still…this is crazy. I'm playing with fire and it needs to stop, and stop immediately. This isn't *like* me."

"What isn't?"

She blew out a breath. "Being around you does something odd to me. I'm not sure how you do it, but you somehow remove all my filters. I don't have sex with men I barely know. I don't yell at people. I certainly don't throw food at them. And yet, in the past few days I've done all of those things. *Why?*"

He lifted his shoulders, unable to tell her. "I like the fact that you're uninhibited."

"Well, I don't. Clearly you're not good for me. And I'm not going to lose my job over you. I'm sorry."

"You won't." He found himself arguing with her. "We'll keep it away from the office. I promise."

"It's a bad idea," she repeated.

"One date," he insisted. "If it's lousy, then I promise I'll back off."

Nikki hesitated. Finally she said, "Adam, I shouldn't

do this, but as I said, you have a strange effect on me. I will go to dinner with you if you promise to leave your cell phone in the car and not think about school."

Not think about school for a whole evening? It sounded really dangerous. And like bliss. "Done," he said promptly. "You have yourself a deal."

"Do you think we can actually have a disaster-free dinner?"

He thought about it. "I don't know," he said truthfully. "We don't have a good track record so far. But I swear I will do my best to make it the most romantic dinner of your life." And he would, too.

Nikki looked pleased by that, if still cautious. "Okay."

He hoped that she would be dessert. Was it bad of him to imagine her in a whipped-cream bikini?

Yeah, that was probably bad. "So, how about this Friday?"

Hey, man, what happened to budgeting four hours of study time first? Friday is only two days away.

"I could pretend to check my calendar," Nikki said. "But then again, I happen to know that I'm free."

"Say, about seven-thirty?"

"Sure. How should I dress?"

"I don't know how to answer that. You'd look good in a barrel with straps."

She smiled at that. "Thanks. Not helpful, but thanks. I'll figure something out."

"Okay, Nikki. I'm looking forward to this very much."

"Me, too," she said.

His Royal Dev-ness wouldn't answer the phone, which took inconvenience to new levels. Adam needed him to delete those pictures, and he needed to borrow money from him.

But was it really borrowing when Dev had a way of forgetting huge bar tabs that got paid for him when he was plastered? He also had a way of forgetting that Adam had helped him move several times, helped him build out the bar that he currently owned and gotten him out of numerous jams over the course of Dev's tumultuous twenty-nine years, one of which had involved duct tape, a ferret and a righteously angry transvestite in a full-length mink.

In short, Dev still owed Adam, not vice versa, and probably would owe him for life.

Devon obligingly returned his call at 3:00 a.m., when Adam had been asleep long enough to slip into REM. "'Lo?" he managed to say, once he'd found the phone.

Raucous background music blistered his ears, even before Dev bellowed, "Dude!" into them.

"Ugh."

"No, no, darlin'—that's illegal in this state," Dev said. "But I sure do like that tiger-striped bra." Clearly he was at a club or party of some kind. "Now, lemme talk to my man Adam, here."

"Not your man," Adam mumbled.

Dev chortled. "When you need my money, you're my man. No two ways about it, beeyotch."

"One of these days, Dev, you're going to regret the way you treat me. One of these days…"

"Yeah, yeah, yeah. Listen, I got your message." His voice dropped, and it sounded as though he'd entered a men's room because of the echo. "You gotta get cash from the bar. I can't wire anything right now."

That sounded ominous. But Adam really didn't want

to know about whatever shady business Dev had going on. "How do I get cash from the bar?"

"It involves the back door, midnight and a pickle jar."

"Forget it. I am not getting arrested."

"Okay, okay, never mind. Let me think a minute." Adam yawned.

"Go to Mark," Dev said, "and—"

"Mark's on his honeymoon, Einstein."

"Right, right…what was I thinking?"

"I don't know."

"Go to Pete. Ask him if he can pay back the G he borrowed from me a couple of months ago. Tell him I asked you to collect it. If he can't come up with it all, tell him that's okay. Take whatever he gives you."

"Okay."

"Great. Do I hear the magic word, buddy?"

"Dev, why should I say the magic word when we have all loaned you money at different times and usually haven't seen a dime of it back? You should say the magic word to *me,* for not making you my own personal cadaver to work on."

"Oh, details," Dev said breezily.

"Yeah, details. Talk to you later, buddy."

"Hey, you get those pics I sent? Pretty hot, huh?"

"Lose them, Dev. I'm serious."

"Ha, ha, ha! Later."

"Later." And Adam hung up the phone, praying that he could go back to sleep.

ADAM SUCCEEDED IN getting five hundred dollars out of Pete, plus his leased BMW Z-4 for the weekend, in exchange for a promise to wash and wax it. He decided to splurge and take Nikki to Azul, a low-key but spectacular restaurant in Miami's Mandarin Oriental.

Though it probably automatically cursed the date, he changed the sheets on his bed and flipped the striped comforter over to the non-grungy, olive-colored side. He even scrubbed the kitchen, took out the garbage and made sure he had two clean, chilled wineglasses for the champagne he stocked in the fridge. They weren't flutes, but they'd have to suffice—if he succeeded in luring Nikki here to the bat cave. Which was a big *if.*

He stuffed most of his books into the bedroom closet, along with the framed photo of a dog that Dev had given him to use for nefarious purposes. Adam shook his head. Dev had actually used it, along with a completely untrue sob story about the dog being run over, to get into the pants of a top fashion model. Worse, he'd then shared the story with pride and made copies of the dog for his buddies to use in similar situations.

Adam showered, shaved and brushed his teeth for twice as long as he usually did. He even slapped on some aftershave. Then he dressed in his best shirt, a pair of dark pants, his good watch and dark shoes. The finishing touch was a pair of criminally expensive prescription sunglasses that he'd bought after winning several hands of poker against Dev. Adam saved them for special occasions, since he didn't want to lose them.

He felt very *GQ* as he strode out of the apartment whistling, tossing his keys up and catching them in his palm. The Beemer completed the picture of a sharply dressed Miami stud out on the town.

Nobody would ever guess that he was reviewing theories of Circulation, Respiration and Regulation in his head as he drove the thirty minutes to Nikki's. He looked *waaay* too cool for school.

When Nikki opened the door to him, he refused to let his mouth drop open like a knucklehead, but he did stand there for a moment, enjoying the picture she presented.

"Hello, gorgeous." It was all he could manage.

"Hi," she said with a slow smile that made everything inside him percolate and steam. "You clean up pretty well yourself."

He lifted a pseudosuave eyebrow and then lowered his glasses, Miami-Vice style, to take her in.

Nikki was gift-wrapped in a silky, cobalt-blue cocktail dress that stopped above the knee. Though it was modest in the front, it did hint at her inviting cleavage through an opening shaped like a little keyhole.

Her hair was blown smooth and straight; it looked infinitely seductive and glamorous in an almost 1940s way. She wore little makeup as far as he could tell— just mascara and a shimmery hot-pink lipstick.

It was when she turned to get her bag and wrap that he almost slid down the doorjamb with his fist in his mouth to block the drool.

Skin: there were smooth, tanned, vast expanses of it. The dress was backless and cut so low that if she'd been wearing even a thong, he'd have seen the top of it.

She wasn't wearing anything underneath. She couldn't have been. And that ass…he remembered that perfect ass very, very well.

As she undulated over to the kitchen counter, the dress moved with her, whispering along her curves and taunting him—as it would taunt every red-blooded man in the restaurant. He wasn't at all sure he wanted to take her out in public in that dress.

And yet it *pretended* to be decent. It pretended to cover her, that wicked swath of silk. That devious creation.

Adam's gaze dropped to her long, bronzed legs and her slender feet, which were lightly criss-crossed with the silver leather straps of a pair of skyscraper heels. Her toenails were painted hot pink, like her lips.

As she rummaged in her evening bag for something, his gaze traveled up to her naked back again, and noted the complete absence of anything resembling a bra under the dress. Now this, this was a mystery and he stepped right up to play detective.

Nikki, as a D-cup kind of girl, had to wear a bra or risk causing traffic accidents and strokes. Yet there was no trace of a strap, and no mark of delineation across the front of the dress, which was made of thin silk. There were no high beams, so to speak, either. Not the slightest indication of nipple showed.

How was this possible?

Adam cocked his head and thought about it. He was still trying to solve the case when she turned around and eyed him quizzically.

"Something wrong?"

"Not at all. Not possible." He reevaluated her more mountainous slopes, still perplexed, if pleasurably so.

"You sure?"

"Positive. I'm just trying to figure something out."

"Care to share?"

He shook his head. Women were very mysterious creatures, but there were certain mysteries that guys shouldn't ask about. They should find out on their own, if and when the time came.

Nikki ran her tongue over her front teeth and shot him a Mona Lisa smile, as if she knew perfectly well what he was trying to figure out. She wasn't stupid, after all, and he hadn't been exactly subtle.

"Shall we?" asked Adam, running a finger around the inside of his collar. He held out his other hand and she placed hers into it. Such a small hand to wield so much power over a man.

They left her apartment and he helped her negotiate the stairs in her high heels, enjoying the flex of her calf muscles with each step. Then he led her to the car and opened her door for her.

"Where's your Mustang?" she asked.

"I thought this ride suited you better," he said smoothly.

"It's beautiful." She bent and then swiveled to lower herself into the Z-4, and he got a tantalizing glimpse of rear cleavage that stole all moisture from his mouth. Suddenly he was too thick-tongued to say, "No, you are." Instead, he made sure her dress was inside the car before closing the door on those mile-long legs.

He rounded the front of the car and got into the driver's side. He double-checked the gas, oil and fluid levels before easing out of the parking lot and into the Miami traffic. Leaving your date by the side of the road while you hitchhiked to a gas station was generally not considered a seductive move.

No sooner had he pulled out than his cell phone rang. "Watch this," he said to Nikki, whose eyes had narrowed. And he pulled it out of his pocket, opened the glove box, and threw it inside. He shut and locked the box. "Happy?"

"Blissful," she said. And she even put her hand on his knee. Adam's hopes for the evening rose.

By the time they pulled into the drive of the Mandarin, her hand had slid higher. The valet-parking attendant was clearly dazzled as he helped Nikki, and only released her hand when Adam cleared his throat and jerked his head in the direction of the car.

The valet dispensed with, Adam slid his hand down Nikki's nude, sun-kissed back to her waist. She shivered with pleasure, and he noted that with equal pleasure.

He felt a little bit like a high-school senior taking the hot girl of his dreams to the prom.

But he repressed the thought. It wasn't smart of him even to remember the kid he'd been in high school, much less step back into his wild, irresponsible shoes.

Then Nikki looked up at him with those green-as-desire eyes of hers, and he fell into them. He forgot about everything but her.

15

AZUL WAS LOCATED INSIDE the Mandarin Oriental Hotel. The restaurant was a serene, sunlit dining experience complete with floor-to-ceiling windows overlooking the bay, white tablecloths and gleaming crystal and silver.

In the center of the place was a white, marble, open kitchen, where guests could watch culinary miracles being shaped to appear on their tables. The staff was unfailingly polite and unobtrusive, and the head chef appeared regularly on national television.

Nikki had never been to a restaurant as nice but as low-key as this one. This hotel was nothing like the glitzy Fontainebleu or the quaint little art-deco hotels along Ocean Drive on South Beach. It had its own clean, modern, Asian flair, not to mention a feeling of peace and space.

The maître d' showed them to a corner table overlooking the water and Adam pulled out Nikki's chair for her. Once he was seated, the host handed them menus and a wine list and said their waiter would be right with them.

Nikki stared, mesmerized, at the water of the bay below and the way the waning sun glittered at the surface. The view was so very Miami: a trompe l'oeil painting of a thousand diamonds on blue, gems that would run through the fingers the moment one's grasp tightened. Sun, sparkle, sex and sin—that was Miami. An intoxicating blend, a Pied Piper's dream, a mirage.

"Would you like a bottle of wine, Nikki?" Adam asked her, smiling at her enjoyment of the view.

"Only if you're planning on drinking at least half of it." She smiled back.

"Red or white? Or champagne?"

"I never turn down champagne." A girl would have to be crazy to do that.

So when the waiter approached, Adam said, "The lady would like champagne."

Nikki liked this *lady* stuff. It made her feel respected and appreciated, almost regal. She straightened her spine and crossed her legs.

The waiter bowed. He pointed to a small section of the wine list, which Nikki couldn't see, so that Adam could make a choice of labels.

"The Taittinger. Very good, sir."

She'd never heard of it, but that was probably a good thing, considering the brands she was familiar with. Those were best mixed with a lot of orange juice and chased with ibuprofen to ward off the instant headache they brought on.

The champagne appeared in a silver bucket, with a white cloth around its royal neck. When poured into flutes, its color was stunning, like antique rose gold.

Nikki thought it was almost too pretty to drink, as the bubbles rose to greet her from its pale, fluid luminescence.

Adam raised his glass, and she followed his lead. "To our first real date," he said. "And to many others."

Hmm. She wasn't at all sure about the *many others* thing. Despite the perfection of the restaurant and the view and his obvious attempts to impress her, she wondered if she really wanted to be with someone whose full attention she'd have for, oh, maybe a couple of hours per week. Aunt Dee's ex must have taken her on nice dates in the beginning, too…and she must have been wildly attracted to him if she'd put up with his schedule.

But Nikki smiled at Adam and drank. The wine was perfectly dry and just sweet enough without being cloying. The bubbles popped seductively on her tongue and then burst, as all bubbles—and fantasies—eventually did.

Well. She wasn't going to worry about the future. She'd enjoy tonight. There was no harm in that, was there? And Margaret wasn't going to walk through the door of Azul and see her fraternizing with Adam.

As they sipped their champagne, the sun streaked the sky with pink and gold, showing off for the diners. Jealous, the clouds added tempestuous violets and purples, while the calm sea reflected the magnificence and then began to drink it down in the west.

Adam's hair looked almost bronze in the fading light. He'd taken off his glasses for a moment while he savored the taste of the champagne, and she studied the blunt, masculine beauty of his face. He had a slightly Roman nose and his hair was a little wavy, curling at the edges. His jaw was strong and his lips sensual. She didn't like men who had what she called lizard lips—meaning very narrow, fleshless ones.

"Do I have a growth?" he asked, with a small smirk.

Startled, she realized she'd been staring. "No! No, I was thinking that you look like some kind of movie star without your glasses on."

He made a choking noise. "You might want to get your eyes checked. Though, come to think of it, I really like that blind quality in you."

"Uh-huh. I notice you're not reaching to put the glasses back on."

"Well, you know. It's nice to be adored. It beats being pelted with cheese and olives," he said dryly.

"Does it?"

"Yes. But I will eventually have to destroy your viewing pleasure and put on my glasses to look at the menu."

"Oh, I like you in the glasses, too," she told him. "They make you look intelligent."

"Ah. Smarter than I really am, you mean?" He winked.

"Most people don't get into med school. So I think you must be brilliant. Just not so much around *women*."

His lips twitched. "I take her to a nice place," he said to nobody in particular. "I buy her champagne. And she pays me backhanded compliments…"

"No, I said you were incredibly smart and I touched on the truth." Was he offended? She couldn't tell.

Adam reached out for his glasses and settled them onto his face again. "Listen, sweetheart, they don't teach a class called Women 101. I can assure you that if one were offered, every guy for miles around—well, every guy except for my buddy Dev—would be wait-listed and dying to get in. Instead, we have to try to figure you out on our own. And some of us don't do such a great job of it."

Nikki laughed.

"Haven't you ever done anything dumb around a guy?" Adam asked.

"Yes. I jumped out of a cake once and smashed my elbow into some poor slob's nose."

"I'm a poor slob," he said to the waiter, who'd returned to take orders for hors d'oeuvres.

"You look very neatly dressed to me, sir," was all the startled man could find to say.

"Thank you. We'd like the oysters, please."

After he'd gone, Nikki added to her list of dumb things. "I got bitten on the butt by savage mosquitoes the size of raptors. And I tried to do a strip tease with clumps of mud and grass stuck to my heels. Other than that, though, I've maintained *total* dignity around men." She laughed and upended her champagne glass.

Adam strong-armed the bottle out of the bucket in spite of the waiter's sudden lunge toward their table to do the same thing. He waved him away and refilled Nikki's flute. "So what you're saying is that we only do stupid things around each other?"

She frowned, nodded and took another sip of the wine. Adam did, too, trying not to imagine her on top of his olive bedspread, wearing nothing but those same tiny bubbles.

"Why do you think that is?" he asked.

"I don't know." She shook her head and looked out over the bay again. "Maybe we're just—" she gestured with her glass "—star-kissed lovers."

"Um, I think that's star-*crossed* lovers," Adam said, struggling to keep a straight face.

"That's what I said."

"Nope. You said star-kissed."

"Oh. Well, doesn't that sound more romantic?" she reasoned.

"No. It sounds like a brand of tuna at the grocery store."

She couldn't help laughing. "Only to a *guy*. To a woman, it's a romantic image, being kissed by stars."

He was puzzled, and probably looked it. "But a star is a burning ball of fire. Any woman it kissed would be instantly incinerated."

She rolled her eyes. "That's scientific, not romantic."

"Yeah, I know. My point exactly...not romantic."

She was laughing at him again. "You really are all guy."

He looked down at himself. "Yes. Last time I checked, anyway."

"Never mind." She sipped again at her champagne. "Enough with the stars. I'd rather be kissed by *you*." She shot him a provocative look from under her lashes.

He stared at her lips. "Is that so?"

"Yes. You've never done that, you know. Kissed me on the lips."

"I haven't?"

"No. Of course, it could be because you thought I was a hook—"

"Let me remedy that right now." And Adam leaned across the table, took her face between his big hands, and ever-so-gently touched his mouth to hers.

"Oh..." she breathed.

And then he turned it into a real kiss, the way a man kisses a woman when he really means it—and he did. He delved into her mouth with his tongue and made a hungry noise, a kind of groan mingled with a growl. And electricity shot from his throat to his toes, shock after shock of it. *Whew*.

"Ohh." She opened her eyes as he released her. He

was pretty sure that it was a good *oh,* as opposed to a bad one.

Adam became gradually aware of their surroundings again. He noted that the waiter was practically dancing a jig with their appetizer plates, not sure whether now was the most opportune time to approach the table.

"Why haven't you ever done that before?" Nikki said to Adam, putting her fingers up to her lips and staring at him.

He shrugged. "Because I'm stupid when it comes to you?"

"Oh, right."

He swallowed convulsively and poured some champagne down his throat to ease the odd tightness there.

"You're a little goofy in fuchsia lipstick," she said. "Not the best look for you."

With a self-conscious laugh, he put his napkin to his lips and wiped it off. "I don't think I did anything to improve your look, either."

Nikki wiped her lipstick off, too, and the effect was unfair. Her nude lips reminded him of the rest of her naked, too. So very, very naked.

Mmm.

And they weren't even through the appetizer stage of dinner yet. Adam looked out at the bay and imagined that it was icy-cold. Then he imagined immersing himself in it. And by the time he added a particularly vicious, flesh-eating Florida lobster to the scenario, his man-part was finally subdued and ready to remain civilized at the table with the rest of him.

Damn it.

In the meantime, he was going to have to watch his luscious, golden-haired date as she nibbled on some morbidly phallic bread sticks—probably whipped up by the chef just to torture him—and downed oysters on the half shell.

"Have one," Nikki prompted him.

"I will." But the truth was that he'd rather have *her*. The image of a tiny Nikki sitting nude, legs crossed and dangling off the edge of one of the little iridescent half shells, entered his mind. He'd probably had too much champagne on an empty stomach, because then he imagined picking her up, King Kong to her Fay Wray....

16

NIKKI FELT ADAM'S EYES on her as she savored one of the crispy oysters, which were wrapped in slivers of beef, tuna and salmon. She didn't know if it was possible to have an orgasm from eating food, but she was sure that she was alarmingly close to having one, right there in front of the waiter, Adam and everyone. The oysters were to die for.

With a bemused smile, Adam took one and began to consume it, a blissful expression crossing his face the moment it entered his mouth. "These are almost better than sex," he said.

She nodded. "Almost."

"But not quite," he said with a grin.

A flash of heat hit her between the legs, so powerful that it almost made her dizzy. That smile of his was as intoxicating as the champagne. A floating sensation traveled through Nikki's veins as she had another oyster.

"So you mentioned a few days ago that your mother has a bakery?" Adam asked, out of the blue. "And you said she needs a new roof?"

"Well, she recently got student loans to go to college, because she never got her degree and always wanted to. So she hired someone and cut back to part-time at the bakery to take classes. And of course the minute she did the mortgage crisis hit and the economy slowed down business and the roof of her house started leaking." Nikki's bliss and buzz began to fade as worry about her mother kicked in again.

"If she got a loan, I'd move in with her to help with the payments, but we really drive each other crazy. She has all of these plants inside and several cats. While I like plants and cats, these particular cats pee in the plants and dig in them and knock them over all the time. So her house smells and there's potting soil everywhere and I can't take it."

Adam wrinkled his nose. "Yeah, I can see how that would be off-putting."

"And she's a book person, while I'm a music and TV person. The sound drives her crazy, especially while she's studying, and I can't always wear headphones...." Nikki shrugged.

"Well, I know someone at a big bank who might be able to get her a lower monthly payment and possibly a home-improvement loan for the roof."

"You do?"

He nodded. "My sister. She's a vice president with SunBelt Securities."

Securities—the word made her think of the *Forbes* article she'd read, *Securities and the Single Mom*. The business idea she'd had was still lodged in her brain. She envisioned a center of some kind, where single moms could get low-cost education and training in different areas—financial planning, avoiding insurance pitfalls, tax accounting, useful business software. Not that she was some kind of guru herself on these matters, but she had a basic knowledge from her B.A. in business. And she could hire people and get grants and subsidies for the women who came in for help.

Aloud she said, "I didn't know you had a sister."

"Now you do. She and my brother are quite a bit older than I am. I was the 'oops' baby after a very festive New Year's Eve." He laughed. "Born on Labor Day, too. The irony did not escape my mom."

Nikki shook her head, smiling.

"Sometimes I kid her that she really named me Damn, but stuck an A on it at the last minute. Because she had to be cussing up a storm when she had me at age forty-three."

"I'm sure she felt very blessed."

"I doubt it," Adam said with a smirk. "I was a real handful."

"But now you'll be the doctor in the family. She must be very proud."

"Well, I had to do something to make up for all the white hair I caused her, right?"

Their entrées arrived, mahi-mahi for Nikki and a lamb dish for Adam. The aromas from both dishes enticed her, and they sampled each other's. She normally didn't care for lamb much, but this was so tender and so good that it melted in her mouth.

Her fish was equally wonderful, light and flaky and served with a subtle, buttery wine sauce that she was sure she'd dream about later.

"So what is your mother studying?" Adam asked, after a few mouthfuls.

"Education," Nikki told him. "She wants to be a teacher."

"That's brave of her."

"Yes, but she'll be a great one. She has endless amounts of patience and she loves kids. She's a natural."

"What grade level?"

"She hopes to teach fourth or fifth grade. That's her favorite age. She says there are too many hormones to deal with after that."

"Very true. So would she close the bakery, then?"

"She's not sure. She's dropped some hints about me taking it over, but I don't think that's for me. I like to bake as a hobby, but doing it professionally is a whole other can of worms."

He nodded.

"So why did you decide to go to medical school, Adam?"

"Probably because I was pre-med in college." He winked.

"Funny. So what made you want to be a doctor?"

He shrugged, turning his wineglass by its stem. "I'm fascinated by the human body—the miracle of how it works and why, sometimes, it stops working so well. And when I was a kid and my grandpa got cancer, I remember telling him that I was going to be a doctor so I could fix him and make it go away."

A lump rose in Nikki's throat at the image.

Adam pressed his lips together and looked with infinite regret over the bay. "Of course, he died before I was even through junior high, but he took me very seriously. He said, 'You do that, Adam. There are a lot of people like me out there who are going to need you. So study hard and pay attention.' And I said, 'Okay, Grandpa. I will.'"

The lump in Nikki's throat grew larger. "So you want to go into oncology?"

"Yes," he said. "Eventually." He looked up at her. "It'll take a while, you know."

He said that with a slight, but very determined smile. She had no doubt that he would follow through. No doubt at all.

They shared a divine chocolate banana cake for dessert, along with top-notch cappuccinos.

"So what are your dreams, Nikki?"

She fiddled with her spoon. "Oh, besides paying off my medical debt, they're pretty ordinary. I don't need to set the world on fire. I grew up with just my mom, and things were hard for her. I guess if anything I'd like to help other women like her. Women who don't have a lot of resources and who are bringing up kids on their own."

"You didn't know your dad?"

Nikki shook her head. "He didn't stay around," she said simply.

"Does that bother you?"

"Sure. Mostly, though, it makes me want two parents for my kids. And I would love to be able to stay home with them and watch them grow."

"And what kind of guy is this other parent, your husband?" He looked at her speculatively.

You. The thought popped into her mind and rattled her. Wow, where did that come from? No, no, no—she was *not* going to be a doctor's starter wife like Aunt Dee. Absolutely not.

She cleared her throat and said with sarcasm, "Well, of course, he'd be a crack addict with no future who beat me daily and sold me on the street corner for his fixes."

"Charming. Can't wait to meet him."

"Yeah, me, either." She stared into Adam's eyes and

he gazed right back at her, his own quizzical and full of humor and a trace of promise.

She looked away first, because the intensity of the eye contact made her squirm. "So. You want kids?"

He nodded.

The odd, expectant silence between them was broken only when the waiter returned to ask if they needed anything else.

"No, thank you," Nikki said.

The waiter nodded, retreated and reappeared with the check. Adam palmed it and paid it with cash. She never saw the total.

He got up and extended his hand to her. "Ready to go?"

She rose and linked her fingers with his. "I don't want this evening to end. That was a wonderful dinner, Adam. Thank you."

"Nobody's ending anything." He squeezed her hand. "We're just beginning."

They walked out of Azul into the spacious hotel and then down to the Mandarin's private beach, a stunning strip of white sand. The wind caught Nikki's hair and toyed with it, blowing it this way and that. She inhaled a breath of fresh air, which was tinged with salt and moonlight, and then bent to slip off her sandals. Her feet settled into the cool sand.

Adam toed off his shoes, too, and took her hand as they strolled along and gazed out at the silvery water. The rhythmic rush, lap and recession of the waves echoed in her ears, an age-old island poetry. The ribbonlike leaves of the royal palms bent and swayed in the breeze, whispering seductively about magic and the moon.

She stopped and drank in the night, dropping her

shoes on the beach. Adam caressed her shoulders and the warmth of his touch had her shivering.

"Cold?" he asked.

She shook her head and turned toward him. He looked taller, darker, more mysterious in the moonlight…so masculine.

It was a given that she'd sleep with him again, despite her big speech about not being a booty call. She was very attracted to him, even if he wasn't a good long-term choice.

He ran both his hands down her nude back, up again to her shoulders and neck, then into her hair. He bent and kissed her as if tasting a delicacy, something exotic.

He slipped inside her mouth, toyed with her tongue, bit her bottom lip gently. "Do you know how much I want you right now?" he said in a low, hoarse voice.

She shook her head.

In answer, he slid his hands down to her hips and then her ass, which he cupped and pulled against him. He was hard against her stomach. "I want to be inside you more than I want to breathe."

Electricity hit all her nerve endings at once.

"I want to pull up your dress and take you right here, standing by the water—make you come until you don't know your name."

She imagined it, her breath coming in shallow, short pants.

"You're not wearing any panties, Nikki. Are you?"

She shook her head.

"So I could do it. I could lift your skirt and slide right into you, and you could ride me—"

"Stop it."

"Why?" His hands released her derriere and then

she felt his thumbs dip under the fabric at either side of her breasts. He unerringly found her nipples and rubbed light circles over them until a sound almost like a sob left her throat and her breath came in ragged bursts.

"Stop, you have to stop…you can't do this to me here."

"I can't?" Adam glanced over his shoulder to see if anyone was paying attention. Then he inched his fingers up the hem of her silk dress, blocking any curious eyes with his own body. He stroked her and the pleasure was so intense that she fell forward against him.

"You're shamelessly wet, Nikki. Tell me what you want."

With a moan, she rubbed herself against his fingers. She couldn't help herself.

"You want me?"

"Yes!"

"Now?"

"Yes!"

He grinned, took his hand away and jerked her skirt down. "Bad girl, Nikki. You're a very bad girl."

She stared at him.

The wicked smile didn't waver. "We can't have sex in public. Are you trying to get us arrested?"

She was so hot that she didn't care about the consequences, and he knew it.

"I'm going put my mouth where my fingers were, honey. And then I'm going to—"

"Get the car," she begged.

And he laughed softly.

"Get the car before I—"

"Before you what, babe? Spontaneously combust?"

17

A BMW Z-4 WAS NO PLACE to have an orgasm. But as Nikki sat in the passenger seat, the powerful engine pulsed an insistent rhythm of vibrations at her core. She was already overstimulated from Adam's beach foreplay, and a little wanton from the champagne.

Their headlong flight to his apartment was marred by several traffic lights, Adam screeching to a frustrated halt at each one.

Nikki shifted in her seat, but the vibrations didn't get any less intense as they squealed up to a stop sign. Adam scorched her with a glance from his side of the car, and she began to feel short of breath again.

"Nikki?"

"Adam, it's the weirdest thing, but I think I'm about to come—"

"No. Oh, no you don't!" He gunned the engine and shot forward.

The accelerated vibrations made things worse. A deep tingle began between her thighs. "But I can't help it…"

"Yes you can. Mind over matter."

She willed the orgasm away, but the intensity in his tone was exciting and made it difficult. She parted her thighs and again shifted in her seat.

Adam burned rubber into his apartment complex and shot into a parking space. He vaulted out of the car, yanked her door open and pulled her out. She couldn't help but laugh.

He hustled her to his door, just about kicked it off its hinges and tugged her inside before slamming it closed. Then he shoved her up against it, dropped to his knees and pushed up her skirt until it was around her waist.

Then his hot, taunting, talented mouth was on her, his hands digging into her inner thighs and his tongue circling her clitoris, then stabbing into her.

Nikki gave a low scream as a hot sea of pleasure engulfed her. Her whole body jerked spasmodically and her head banged back against the door. She would have fallen if not for Adam's hands holding her up. And still, relentlessly he added to the intensity until she came apart a second time.

Finally he stopped, lifted her and absconded with her into his bedroom. He stripped off her dress, slipped off her sandals and laid her on the bed. She was vaguely aware that he put on a condom.

Then he slid into her, all the way home, and she loved the fullness, loved the way he seemed to lose his own sanity almost immediately and give in to the laws of pure pleasure.

"Too fast, too fast," he murmured, and pulled almost all the way out of her. "But I solved the mystery."

"What mystery?" She ran her hands over the smooth, taut skin of his shoulders and beautifully sculpted chest. She slid them down his muscular arms, covered his hands with her own.

"The mystery of how you wore that dress without a bra."

"It's built-in, silly."

"Never knew they could do that." He buried his face between her breasts and slid back into her with a deep groan. Then he toyed with her nipples, sucking first one and then the other into his mouth.

A medical student couldn't figure out the lining in a dress? It wasn't heart surgery. But she laughed. "As long as you can do *this,* then it's okay," she said.

"Mmm. I can do this very well."

"Yes."

"And this. And this, too…"

"Ohh."

"You see, I've studied anatomy."

"And what was your favorite part of the body?"

He drove into her, hard, and she squeaked. "I'm inside it right now." He chuckled.

But the chuckle didn't last very long. It soon gave way to ragged breathing as he built to his climax. This time she wasn't along for the ride, but she took pleasure in his pleasure, in the minute muscular shifts of his body and the pounding of his heart. He drove harder and faster, and she arched her back and lifted herself off the bed to meet him and maximize their contact. She reached down to the underside of his cock and put two fingers against it, increasing the friction and sensation for him.

And he came almost violently, jerking spasmodically inside her. She gave a smug, feminine sigh and wrapped her legs more tightly around him.

"I think I may have just died," he said, collapsing onto her.

She smiled in the darkness. "Then evidently you died a pretty happy guy."

"Oh, *yeah,*" he said. "A lucky one, too."

And he kissed her.

ADAM PUT ON SOME MUSIC—Vampire Weekend—and they drank more champagne. It was there, after all, and so were they. He was glad he'd chilled the glasses beforehand, and Nikki didn't care at all that they were for wine and not champagne.

"Champagne glasses are a little frustrating," she told him. "They don't hold more than three or four mouthfuls."

"Ah, yes…" he said in a terrible accent. "Ze French, zey think champagne should be sipped." He mock-demonstrated, pinky flared out.

She laughed. "Well, I'm American and I like to *drink* it."

He raised his eyebrows. "Would you prefer a pilsner glass, then? I have one that will hold about half the bottle."

She punched him playfully.

They talked.

And talked.

And talked some more…about everything from the Miami Dolphins to new research on a cancer drug, from movies they loved—his favorite was *Inside Job;* hers was *The Thomas Crown Affair*—to the best ice cream: Ben & Jerry's versus Häagen-Dazs.

Nikki asked him for some ice water. "I have to stop drinking champagne, or my head will hate me in the morning."

He laughed. "No, honey, you have to stop drinking champagne because it's *gone.*"

She gasped. "Did we finish a whole other bottle?"

He nodded, wincing. He thought of his own probable champagne headache and how it would affect his concentration on his books tomorrow. Shit. He looked at his watch and saw that somehow, it had gotten to be almost two o'clock in the morning. So much for the four hours he'd allotted for the date.

"Is it past your bedtime?" Nikki asked, her tone light.

"Um." He kissed her nose. "Yeah, kind of. I have to hit the books all day tomorrow. I should take you home."

She was silent. "I could stay, and you could take me in the morning."

Stay? As in overnight? That was very…girlfriend-like. And girlfriends needed a lot of time and attention and TLC. And he had so very little time. This was complicated. He hadn't really thought beyond this date tonight. He wanted her to stay, but he would also need her to be gone in the morning.

No third chances, he reminded himself. *You can only screw up your future once. The girl is gorgeous and sweet and funny and sexy—and a giant distraction that you cannot afford.*

But Nikki was looking at him expectantly and he realized he had to say something. *Now.*

He tucked a curl behind her ear. "That's the best offer I've had all night, but I have to warn you—I'll get up at six to run." There, that should do the trick. She'd be outta here.

"Six?" She was horrified. But she still didn't ask him to take her home. "Don't wake me."

So she was staying. Adam tried to figure out how he felt about that. He yawned again and decided he was too tired for emotional introspection. He got up and extended his hand to her. "Okay, princess. You can sleep in."

NIKKI TOLD HERSELF that she was imagining things. That Adam didn't really want to be rid of her. That he was just tired and had tried to be a gentleman by offering to take her home.

Still, she couldn't quite shake off the feeling that he didn't want her there. She slept nude, and so did Adam. He kissed her—see, she was being silly—and then trailed his fingers down her body until he got to the little heart of hair at her mons. He was still fascinated with that, it seemed. Well, he'd better enjoy it while he could, because she was never going through that kind of sadistic torture again.

If nature had put hair there, there must be a good reason for it, even if that reason was mysterious. She drifted off to sleep with the scent of Adam's skin in her nostrils and the warmth of him against her.

She awoke two hours later, dying of thirst. She slipped out of bed and felt her way out of his room and into the kitchen, where she found the light switch on the wall and flipped it on. She found a big plastic cup in a cabinet and filled it with cold water from the dispenser on the refrigerator, then gulped deeply as she looked around.

Adam's apartment was furnished in Utilitarian Grad Student, with a mismatched sofa and chair and a racing bike and beige carpet and not a single plant. The most luxurious item in the place was the entertainment system, a flat-screen TV with stereo equipment. But even that was a brand she'd never heard of. A photo stood on an end table. It was of Adam and his family at the Grand Canyon. They all looked physically fit and breezily happy, without a care in the world. Nikki felt a pang of envy.

Her mother was under constant stress and had put on fifty pounds over the past few years. Of course, she spent her days making high-calorie pastries and cakes and breads. And despite Nikki's nagging, she drank very little besides coffee. Nikki thought of the dizziness again and worried.

She drank every ounce of the water from the huge cup, and felt better. She wandered over to a corner desk that Adam had set up in the nook between the kitchen and living area. It was stacked with books and papers and binders of more paper. The books had titles like *Metabolism and Reproduction, Host & Defense* and *Foundations of Medicine*. They were fat and intimidating. She lifted the cover of the top one and took it over to the light, where she flipped through it. Medical and scientific jargon filled the pages, making her cringe.

Suddenly the ice-maker in Adam's fridge churned out several cubes, making her jump. She dropped the book, which landed on her toes, and she couldn't help a yelp of pain.

"Nikki?" called Adam, sleepily.

"Uh, hi. Sorry. I was looking at one of your books and dropped it."

He came out of the bedroom, yawning and rubbing at his face. Though his hair stuck up in strange tufts and he had sheet marks on his face, he looked like any woman's fantasy.

Broad, muscular shoulders topped a ripped chest with just enough hair to look masculine without the woolly bear factor. His belly was flat and cut with muscle. His hips were narrow, and…well, what lay between them was only semi-dormant.

Adam was hung.

As he took in her naked body while she still clutched the book, he came more fully alert. So did the rest of him, and she stared, fascinated.

He grinned at her. "What are you doing with my *Metabolism and Reproduction* book? Studying at 4:30 a.m. is *my* thing."

She shrugged and held up the cup. "I couldn't sleep, and I was thirsty."

"Hey, beautiful. Stop snooping and come 'ere."

"I wasn't snooping!"

"Uh-huh." He moved forward on those long, graceful, athletic legs of his and twitched the book out of her hands. Then he easily picked her up and threw her over his shoulder.

"What are you—"

He smacked her bottom.

"—doing?" she squeaked.

"Playing caveman and dragging you off to my lair to have my wicked way with you." He walked with her into the bedroom and dropped her unceremoniously onto the covers. Then he pinned her wrists with his hands and kissed her while nudging her thighs apart with his knee.

"You're one insatiable caveman," she said once she could get some air.

"Ugg," Adam replied. "Now, let me show you my club."

"I've seen it," she reminded him.

"Let me show it to you again."

And without much further notice, he entered her,

slowly but powerfully, pushing inward until she felt she could feel him up to her neck.

"Nikki," he breathed into her ear. "You're so sweet, so hot, so tight. I want to stay inside you forever."

Though rationally she knew there might be practical problems with that, physically it sounded perfect right now. Then he moved infinitesimally, rubbing himself against a spot that felt particularly good, and she forgot all about anything rational or logical…she relinquished control to the man and the moon.

18

NIKKI AWOKE TO THE SMELL of fresh coffee. She opened her eyes to a pale, silvery light creeping through the edges of Adam's blinds, and rolled toward his side of the bed, but he wasn't there.

He must be in the kitchen. She yawned and forced herself upright, wincing a little at her inevitable champagne headache. She slid out of bed and put on his discarded shirt from the night before. Then she walked into the kitchen to find it empty.

"Adam?" she called.

True to his word, he must have gone running. Nikki wrinkled her nose. A person who went running at—she glanced at the clock on his microwave oven—5:53 a.m., after partying until 2:00 a.m., qualified as a borderline alien. She made a mental note to check his skin for a green tinge and make sure his ears weren't pointed when he returned.

Then she went back to bed.

She woke about forty minutes later when Adam came through the bedroom door, his hair and T-shirt sopping wet, smelling like a ripe foreign cheese. "Still asleep, huh?" he panted.

Why did she suddenly feel like a fat garden slug? "Yeah, like most people early on a Saturday morning," she said, trying her best to keep any acid out of her voice.

Adam stripped off his sweat-soaked shirt and neatly shot it, basketball-style, into the dirty-clothes basket in the far corner of his room. "Carpe diem," he said, winked and headed for the shower.

Nikki stared after him. "Carpe my left butt cheek," she muttered, and pulled the covers up over her face to block out the light. She wondered if he had any ibuprofen for her aching head, but then decided that she was too lazy to get it even if he did. She rolled over and stuffed her head under the pillow.

All too soon, she could hear him pulling open drawers with far too much energy, getting dressed and then banging around in the kitchen. This morning-person thing of his was an *extremely* unattractive habit.

She was snoozing again, dreaming that she'd dropped a sleeping pill into his nightcap, when a clunk sounded on the bedside table next to her head.

"I thought you might like some coffee," Adam's voice boomed.

She opened her eyes and squinted at the mug that stood in front of her. "Um. Thanks."

"No problem."

He stood there for a moment, looming over her and clearly expecting her to pop out of his bed like a jack-in-the-box.

She didn't.

"Well," he said, shifting from one foot to the other. "I'll, uh, just be in the other room, okay?"

She nodded.

"There's shampoo and stuff in the shower if you want to clean up."

No offense, but my head hurts and I'm tired and for the moment, I'm totally happy just being lazy and dirty. But Nikki didn't say it aloud. "Okay," she mumbled.

Adam evidently gave up, because the next time she opened her eyes he was gone and the coffee he'd brought her was cold. She staggered with it into the kitchen and stuck it in the microwave to heat it through.

Adam—or a stone facsimile of Adam—sat on the couch with his head bent over another monster textbook.

"Hi," she said.

The statue grunted and made a note on a legal pad.

"I slept well, thanks." She took a sip of the now-warm-again coffee. "You?"

"Uh-huh. Gimme a second, okay?"

"Sure." Nikki took another sip of stale coffee.

The second turned into a minute, and then another. Finally she wandered into the living room and sat in the chair opposite Adam while he continued to read and make notes. She was aware of being an attractive blonde, naked under his shirt, but she felt like an old, stained potholder forgotten next to the stove.

Well. This was fun. "What are you studying?" Nikki asked.

"Just gimme a second," Adam said for the second time, without looking up at her.

Nikki drained her coffee and disappeared to take a shower, all without him seeming to register her presence. She washed the traces of him off her body, sore from last night, and wondered if she'd imagined the tenderness and care he'd shown.

She told herself to grow up—he was a busy medical student and clearly had a lot to do. She told herself it wasn't personal, that his focus had just shifted from fun to work.

But the fact was that it *felt* personal.

She got out of the shower, wrapped herself in a towel and went in search of the dress she'd worn last night. It lay discarded in front of Adam's door, looking as hungover and moody as she was.

Deliberately, she dropped the towel so that she stood naked, four yards from Adam. But even nudity failed to get his attention. So she sighed and pulled on the dress, feeling very much like Cinderella after the ball.

Adam was oblivious, still engrossed in his book, so she cleared her throat.

He looked up, glanced at his watch and asked, "Ready?"

"Sure." So much for a leisurely, loving breakfast with the newspaper and maybe some bagels.

Nikki picked up her purse and shoes. She followed him out the door, feeling dismissed.

She kept her eyes closed during the drive because pretending to be sleepy was better than being forced to make conversation with Adam, whose head was so clearly somewhere else.

When they pulled up outside her apartment, she summoned a smile and said, "Thank you, Adam. I had a great time." She hesitated, then leaned over and kissed his cheek before she got out of the car.

"I did, too," he said.

An awkward pause ensued.

"Really, it was fantastic. I'll call you, okay?"

He didn't mention when. Later today? Next month? A year from now?

"Okay." She slid out of the car and gave him a little wave before she walked to the stairs that led to the second level of her complex.

He waved back and drove away.

As she climbed the stairs, Nikki told herself to put it all out of her mind. But it was hard. Somewhere, somehow, there had been a psychological shift between them, and she'd gone from object of desire to object of…good riddance? Maybe that was too strong a term. Maybe Adam was just dog-tired and overworked and she was imagining things.

But the sudden closeness they'd shared followed by the sudden distance this morning made no sense to her. She didn't know what to think.

You know he's wrong for you, she told herself. *So why worry about it?*

A girl like her, who had grown up without a father, needed more from a guy than this hot-and-cold treatment. She needed a guy who would be both emotionally and physically present in her life.

So she'd pull up her big-girl panties—once she had some panties back on—and get over Adam Burke.

ON MONDAY MORNING, as Nikki stood making photocopies at work, an older man opened the door from the hallway, peering around a large vase of pink roses.

"Looking for a Miss Nikki Fine," he mumbled.

"Oh. That's me."

The scent of the flowers wafted across the room, a sweet, grassy-woodsy scent that masked the normal vinyl, industrial-carpet and metallic file-cabinet smell.

"Then these are for you, ma'am." He set them on her desk and produced a paper. "If you'll sign right here to show you received them."

She scribbled her signature, her heartbeat coming faster. They were from Adam. She knew it.

So what? she asked herself.

Dear Nikki,
Thank you for the most romantic evening of my life.
XOXO, Adam.

Her heart rolled over like a dog for a belly scratch and thumped its tail. *See? You're an idiot. He was tired yesterday morning and had to study.*

Then she wanted to strangle herself. *You're moving on, remember?* Flowers don't change the facts.

But clearly, her heart didn't want to move on.

Feeling crazy, she kissed the tiny card and tucked it into her bra—unfortunately just as Margaret came in.

"Good morning, Margaret. How was your weekend?" asked Nikki, as she blushed and straightened her sweater.

Margaret raised her eyebrows, then glared at the roses as if they'd spat on her. "Fine," she said. "Who are those for?"

"Me."

Margaret managed to look even more offended, and directed a suspicious glance at Nikki, as if to ask her how she'd earned them. Then she turned her beady black eyes to the flowers again. Surprisingly, they didn't wither and blacken. "How nice," was all Mags could dredge up to say.

Nikki was glad that she didn't ask who they were from. She'd have had to lie because of the whole fraternization-with-students issue.

Fraternize? Oh, no. Not her. She was the model employee. She certainly had not woken up naked in a student's bed on the weekend. Huh-uh. Who could suspect such a thing?

Maggie Mae stomped off to terrorize someone else, and Nikki heaved a sigh of relief. She fingered the card from Adam, smiled, and dialed his number on her cell phone to thank him. No answer. Well, he was probably in class and she'd try again later.

Nikki worked until lunchtime and then tried again as she headed out for a salad. She left a message this time. "Adam, it's Nikki. Thank you so much for the gorgeous roses. Call me or stop by after one, okay? Bye."

One small Greek salad with extra feta consumed, Nikki headed back to work. As she turned down the hall that led to the dean's office, she saw Trammel himself standing with Margaret at the big bulletin board where students posted fliers for group activities, ads for roommates and announcements.

His normally pleasant face looked thunderous, and as she approached he shook his head in disgust. He started to turn toward the office and then caught sight of her out of the corner of his eye.

"You," he said, "are fired. Pack your things."

The words hit her like a brick in the face. *"Wh-what?"*

He gestured at the bulletin board and then looked her up and down. He shook his head again. Then he turned on his heel, stalked to the office door and wrenched it open, slamming it shut behind him.

While Nikki stood there with her mouth open, knees shaking, he opened the door and stuck his head out again. "Margaret, please clean those up and get rid of them." The door slammed for a second time.

"What is going on?" Nikki's voice trembled as she

asked the question. Then she forced her feet forward and took a look at the bulletin board. Her own image was everywhere—and *not* clad in conservative business attire. Horrified, she stopped breathing.

"I think you can answer that question better than we can," Margaret snapped, pulling thumbtacked photographs off the board. She thrust a couple of them at Nikki and kept at it.

Nikki looked down at the pictures.

They were of her and Adam.

On the night of the bachelor party.

He was on the floor, clutching his nose and staring up in bemusement. She had bent forward over him, and the shot was all cleavage. Fearsome amounts of it.

The next shot had been taken from a salacious angle behind her as she straddled him, asking if he was okay. It left very little to the imagination.

Blood rushed to Nikki's face, pulsing so hard that it felt as if it were boiling. Panic and horror knocked her in the stomach. How had these gotten here?

Margaret slapped more photos into her hands, and they didn't get any better. Who had taken them?

One more photo, of a bare-bottomed, thong-clad Nikki leaving with Adam, was the icing on her giant pink slip. And the last thing Mags threw at her was a long, bannerlike strip of paper emblazoned with the words:

WHAT'S UP, DOC? Is that a tongue depressor in his pocket or is Adam Burke just happy to see this babe?

Nikki's legs threatened to give way, and she clutched at the wall behind her. She couldn't decide whether to throw up or to kill herself.

Months. Months of applications and office-skills tests and rounding up recommendation letters…months of waiting and cheerful follow-up phone calls to say she was so enthused about the job and really wanted it, please not to forget her…all down the drain.

Her salary, down the drain.

Her benefits, down the drain.

Her *health insurance*—down the drain.

Nikki slid down the wall and sat on the cold, mass-produced tile, the photos still clutched in her hands.

Fired.

Without this job, she couldn't pay her rent or clear her debt. She couldn't feed herself. And she now couldn't help her mother finance the new roof.

Fired. Not for *job* performance, but for a *bachelor party* performance.

She wasn't sure how long she sat there, but two things happened simultaneously after a block of time had gone by. One, Margaret emerged with a cardboard box containing stuff from her desk drawers, the roses, her purse and a mug she'd brought for coffee. And two, Adam came around the corner with a backpack hitched over his shoulder.

Margaret thumped the box down at her feet and said, "You cannot sit there. If you're not gone in two minutes, I will call security to escort you from the building." Then Mags caught sight of Adam. "And *you,*" she said, pointing a long, bony finger at him, "are a disgrace! You can forget about the Perez scholarship, young man."

Adam opened and then closed his mouth as she stomped into the office. He looked at Nikki. "What the hell? Why are you sitting on the floor? What's her problem? What's going on?"

Nikki, now trembling uncontrollably, somehow managed to get to her feet. She threw the photos and the horrible paper banner at him. Then she grabbed her purse and the cup and kicked the box at him as hard as she could.

"Nikki! What— Oh, *Jesus*. Oh, *no*...Nikki, *wait!*"

Why wouldn't her lungs work? She ran blindly anyway. Down the hallway and the stairs, past a startled woman at the door and the guy with the drink cart outside.

She gave a ragged gasp and a prayer for air, and opened her mouth simultaneously to scream. She didn't know which she wanted to do first, but the air took precedence and the scream stayed silent. Nikki started to hyperventilate as Adam caught up to her and took her arm.

She shook him off, unable to speak to him even if she'd wanted to. She tried to process her necessities and impulses at the same time, but her brain wasn't helping. Breathe, puke, scream, hit Adam, run, breathe, kill self, puke, kill Adam, breathe, scream...

Why, every time she let down her guard around him, did he let *her* down? What was this crazy repeat pattern of theirs? This was probably how her mom had ended up pregnant and alone—by letting someone get close whom she *knew* wasn't right for her.

"Nikki," he said, his voice insistent.

"No," she said.

"Nikki—"

She finally sucked in some air. "Get away from me!"

"Breathe," he told her, steering her to a bench. "Sit down and put your head between your knees. Breathe."

"Do. Not. Touch. Me."

"Fine," he said. "Now *breathe!*"

She found herself following Dr. Burke's orders. She bent forward, parallel with the ground, and sucked in air as she watched an ant scurry across the concrete sidewalk. The ant had more purpose than she did now. The ant probably got some kind of ant pay and benefits from his anthill. She moved her foot so he could get by more easily on whatever mission he'd been assigned.

"You okay?" Adam asked, his hand hovering over her back but afraid to touch her. She could see it out of the corner of her eye.

She shook her head.

"Did they fire you?"

She nodded.

"I had nothing to do with this."

"Right." She straightened and got to her feet.

"I didn't. And I'm so sorry, Nikki—"

She just looked at him, and he fell silent. His expression was grim.

"I know who put these up—my friend Dev, who likes to play jokes on people. And I'm going to go beat the crap out of him."

"Like I care. Is that going to pay my rent or clear my debt? Is that going to help finance my mom's roof?"

"Nikki, I'll fix this."

The laughter out of her mouth didn't even sound like her own. "Don't bother. Just stay away from me, Adam. Keep the hell out of my life, what's left of it." Nikki got to her feet unsteadily and brushed off the back of her skirt.

"You blow hot," she said. "You blow cold. One minute I'm a princess, the next I'm persona non grata. You make me into a crazy person. I don't even recognize myself with you in my world! I'm not an emotional roller coaster. I'm not impulsive. I've always been practical…except when *you're* around. I've become a disaster since I met you, and I'm not okay with that."

He looked stricken.

She threw her purse over her shoulder and thought about hitting him over the head with the coffee mug, but couldn't summon the energy. Besides, a little voice in the back of her head—not a crazy one, an all-too-sane one—told her that if she hadn't been dumb enough to let Yvonne put her in that position and in those "clothes," she wouldn't be starring in skanky photos. She'd never have met Adam, or Dev for that matter.

The thought didn't bring her any comfort.

"Nikki—"

She put one foot in front of the other and started walking away from the guy of her fantasies…who'd somehow become the guy of her nightmares. "*Goodbye,* Adam."

19

ADAM CURSED UNTIL HE couldn't think of any more curse words. Then he repeated them all until he ran out of breath, and growled them in different, more imaginative sequences as he drove his car straight to Devon's fancy-ass white high-rise on Brickell in the heart of fashionable Miami.

Devon had unwisely given him an elevator code and a key about a year ago when Adam was staying with him and looking for his own apartment near the university. The same guy still worked at reception, and waved him in.

Up Adam went in the elevator, all the way to the twenty-first floor, with the crumpled photos and banner in his backpack. He got out of the elevator, removed them and headed for unit 2122. It was only 1:30 p.m., and Dev stayed at his bar until it closed around 4:00 a.m., so he'd still be asleep.

But not for long.

Adam unlocked the door and kicked it closed behind him. He stalked straight to the bedroom where he threw open the door and then pulled open the blinds.

Dev rolled over with a groggy moan. "Wha fah?"

Adam grabbed Dev by the neck and yanked him to a sitting position before plowing his fist into his jaw.

Naturally, Dev lay back down again, a little more quickly than he'd probably intended.

Adam stuffed one of the photos into his open mouth, and followed it with another one.

"Gah! Whah ra ooig?"

"What am I doing? I'm feeding you those friggin' pictures you plastered outside the dean's office, you asshole!"

Adam shoved another photo into Dev's mouth, at which point Dev came awake enough to try to defend himself. He lurched forward, head-butting Adam in the gut and knocking him off the bed.

Adam rolled, found his feet again and launched himself back at Devon. He plowed into him with the full force of his body, rolled him onto his stomach and sat on him, wrenching one of his arms behind his back. "You jackass!" Adam yelled. "Did you even stop to think what the consequences of your little gag might be?"

Dev bellowed into the bedcovers and tried to buck him off. He failed.

"Did you?"

Another bellow.

"Do you realize that Nikki *works* in the friggin' dean's office? She got fired because of you. And I lost out on the Perez scholarship because of this stunt."

Adam was afraid he'd kill Dev if he didn't put some distance between them, so he gave him a final cuff on the back of the head and then propelled himself to the other side of the room.

Dev rolled over, gasped and coughed. Then he eloquently dropped an F-bomb.

"That's it? That's all you got?"

"I didn't think—"

"How 'bout one hell of an apology, man?"

Dev struggled to a sitting position, rubbed at his jaw and actually managed to look remorseful. "Dude. I'm sor—"

"Don't call me *dude,* you piece of shit."

"Adam. I'm sorry. I had no clue."

"Well, it's about time you got one. Maybe even two or three."

"I didn't know Nikki worked there. How could I?"

Adam glared at him. "You're going to make this up to her, and you're going to make it up to me, too."

Dev nodded. "Yeah, I will. How?"

Adam eyed him scathingly, from his stupid, product-laden hair to his flashy gold chain to his idiotic boxers with surfing pigs on them. "I'll tell you exactly how. You, Dev, are a Photoshop expert."

"Uh. I am?"

"Yes. As of this moment, you are. And you are going to accompany me to the dean's office this afternoon, and you are going to explain to him exactly how you used Photoshop to put Nikki's head onto a stripper's body, and my head onto the guy's."

"O-kaay..." Dev said dubiously.

"And then you are going to most humbly apologize to the dean, and say that you are the biggest wanker on the planet, and you are going to beg him on your knees for Nikki's job back. Then you are going to beg him to put me back in the running for the Perez scholarship. Do you understand?"

Dev nodded.

Adam crossed the room and yanked open his closet doors.

"What are you doing, man?"

"You are going to wear a plain, white shirt. You are going to take off that gold chain. And you are not going to put that grease-crap in your hair. You will part it on the side like the preppiest kid ever to descend from the Mayflower families. You will not wear eight ounces of Latin-lover cologne. You will not wear that flashy, in-your-face Rolex—"

"Jeez. Do you want to tell me how to wipe my ass, too?"

"No. You will not be wiping your ass. You will be kissing the dean's. Got it?"

"Sure," Dev said glumly.

"And when we leave there and you've done your job with him, then we're going to go to Nikki's place and you can kiss hers, not that it will do me any good now." Adam dropped his head into his hands.

Dev said nothing for a long moment. Then, "You care about her."

Adam lifted his head and skewered his friend with a look.

"Oh, man, oh, man. I've really screwed up, haven't I?"

"You *dick*head," Adam said. And then he followed it with every other bad word he could think of.

Dev staggered to his feet and headed for the shower.

"Yes, I care about her," Adam told him. "You degenerate pig." He dropped his head into his hands. "And I should walk away now, because I can't give her the time and attention that she deserves." He groaned. "But I can't walk away. There's something about her, a grace or a...a...peace with herself that I don't have. I tap into that. I relax around her. Like a cat in a pool of sun-shine."

"Dude," Dev said, holding up a hand and looking faintly nauseated.

"And she bakes stuff that's out of this world. My mom? She can burn water."

"Next you're going to tell me that Nikki feels like your heart's true home," Dev said, squinting at him.

"Yes." Adam was astonished. "That's exactly it. How did you come up with that?"

Dev closed his eyes and shook his head.

"Oh. I thought for a minute there you'd been taking a poetry class or something. I should have known you were being sarcastic, you bastard."

"Moi?"

Adam rolled his eyes. "Fine. So I'll mock you when it happens to you—*if* it ever happens to you."

"Photoshop," Dev muttered, changing the subject. "Wait. You know who can help us fix this?"

"Who?"

"Remember Evan Underwood? They used to call him Enzo?"

"What about him?"

"His cousin Hal owns Underwood Technologies and I'll bet he could create some 'original' photos for us. You know, the ones that I supposedly doctored."

"You think?"

"Yeah. Give me twenty-four hours, okay? And I swear I'll fix this for you."

Adam mulled it over.

"I'm really, really sorry, man. I meant this as a prank. I was just razzin' you."

Adam shielded his eyes so he didn't have to look at Dev anymore in those Windex-blue boxers with the surfing pigs on them. "Dev, you've got exactly twenty-four hours. If you fail me, then you and I are going to have a hot boating date with some rope and some cinder blocks. Got it?"

Dev sprinted for Evan's number.

THE TEARS DIDN'T COME for Nikki until she was in her car, thank God. Behind the tinted glass of the Beetle's windshield, she could leak and sniffle for the entire drive home.

Fired.

All because she'd met Adam.

She'd used the term *star-kissed lovers* in Azul, but at this point she felt more as if they were star-*crapped* lovers. Except that she'd never be his lover again. She thought it with bravado, but the idea only made her cry harder.

What kind of guy had friends who would do this?

The kind of guy who would try to pay her for sex. The kind of *jerk* who would look at his cell phone in the middle of the act. The kind of *pig* who wallowed with other pigs.

They probably got together with other slimeballs on the weekends and watched porn involving sick toys and animals. Who knew—maybe they threw parties and passed around hookers like joints.

Nikki angrily banished the little voice inside her that insisted Adam was not that kind of person. How could she know what kind of person he really was? After all, nobody had dreamed that other nice-looking med student was the Craig's List Killer.

Maybe Adam was the Bachelor Party Beast, and went around ruining amateur strippers' lives.

The little voice inside told her not to be stupid.

Too freaking late! she snapped back.

She'd been stupid on so many levels. Taking the gig, for one. Allowing pictures to be taken. Going back to Adam's hotel room—that actually ranked highest on the Moron List. No. Falling in love with him did.

The thought caused Nikki to stomp on her brakes at a green light, which the drivers behind her did not seem to appreciate. Honks and beeps and hand gestures ensued. Cussing in Spanish followed.

No, no, no, no, *nooo.* She had not fallen in love with Adam. That was a crazy idea. You didn't fall in love with someone you'd only known for a week, after all. That was ridiculous.

The stupid little voice inside her tried to get all logical and rational. It asked where was the rule book that established how long one had to know a person before falling in love?

Nikki told the little voice to go to hell.

It responded with affronted snarkiness that it was already there.

Was it saying that being trapped in her brain was hell?

Well, that was the first sensible thing the voice had said all week.

Nikki congratulated it.

Then she stepped hard on the gas pedal and rocketed toward home, because if she stayed out on the street like this, trading barbs with a little voice in her hellhead, she would definitely get picked up and packed into a little white cell lined with padding so that she couldn't hurt herself.

She also cried harder. Yeah…that was good. Maybe she could drown the voice in her sorrows.

Finally she turned into her apartment complex,

blinking away the tears. She sat there in her car for a moment, wishing that it was a magic car that could drive to the nearest grocery store to get her a giant tub of rocky-road ice cream and a big bag of cherry Twizzlers, too. And while it was at it, the Beetle could stop and get her some of those wonderful old movies with Audrey Hepburn and Cary Grant and Grace Kelly and Jimmy Stewart.

Movies where the heroine's problems were easily solved and the men in her life were wonderful, witty, dapper and handsome. They made perfect martinis and would never offer to pay her for sex or be friends with anyone who would plaster naked pictures up at her place of employment.

But though her Beetle was adorable, it was not magic—and she couldn't even be mad at it for its lack of supernatural gifts.

Nikki rested her forehead on the steering wheel and gave in to fresh sobs. Then she forced herself out of the car, up the stairs to her apartment, and called her mom.

20

"MOM, EVEN IF I TAKE OVER here and keep things running, I'm going to have to move in with you," Nikki said as she stood in the kitchen of Sweetheart's and folded fresh blueberries into the batter for a huge batch of muffins.

She wore a baggy shirt, aerobics shoes and her oldest pair of jeans. They sported holes in both knees and had frayed and faded at the back where she'd stepped on them and dragged them on the floor, since they'd always been too long for flat shoes.

Despite her care, some of the blueberries broke, creating blue streaks in the mixture. Well, the blue streaks were a metaphor for how she felt, so there.

"And that still doesn't change the fact that now neither one of us can afford health insurance. That was one of the big reasons I wanted to work for the university—they pay for that."

"Well, honey, you know you're always welcome at home, and we just have to pray that neither one of us gets sick."

Tara was covered from neck to knees in a white

apron over her own T-shirt and jeans. Her only jewelry was a pair of tiny chocolate-doughnut earrings with multicolored sprinkles that Nikki had given her last Christmas. They were inexpensive and made out of painted resin, but she adored them.

"Mom, praying that you stay healthy is sticking your head into the sand."

Tara rolled her eyes. "Oh, ye of little faith. And better my head in the sand than your fanny in a G-string, honeybun."

Ouch. Low blow. "Mom, can we please not talk about that?" Unfortunately she'd been so upset that she'd spilled everything.

Her mother giggled.

"Stop it," ordered Nikki.

"Sorry, just picturing your gran's face if she could have seen you. It would have made my out-of-wedlock pregnancy pale in comparison. And you don't even know how much trouble I got in for that."

Nikki had heard the story many times. How Gran and Poppy had kicked Tara out of the house, but Poppy had run out the screen door and stood behind his little girl's car before she could even back out of the driveway.

They'd unloaded her car, unpacked her suitcases and held her while she cried. Then Gran had gone about getting Tara the best medical care available and told the neighbors to mind their own business. Poppy had cleaned his gun and gone to talk to "that young hound," much good did it do anyone.

The "hound" spent most of his flea-bitten life stoned out of his gourd and could barely support himself, much less a wife and a baby. Gran and Poppy decided that rather than have their grandchild grow up with that poor excuse of a father, they'd have him sign a nice little legal document, and Tara agreed, letting her knight in dusty black leather ride his third-hand Harley off into the sunset without her.

"Yeah, well," said Nikki. "I'm only carrying on a family tradition of scarlet women. We're just degenerates, aren't we?"

"Pretty much," said Tara cheerfully. "You know, compromising the good citizens' health with evil sugar and all that." She bustled around, setting the trays of cookies, pastries, doughnuts, cakes and pies inside the display cases.

Once everything had been set out, she wiped her hands on her apron and turned to face Nikki. "In all seriousness, sweetie, I want you to stop worrying about me. God will take care of my health. And God will find a solution for the roof, too."

Nikki sighed. "Okay. But I think the Big Guy would want you to be, um, very proactive in these matters. So at least go see a real doctor about the dizzy spells. Remember, God helps those who help themselves, right?"

Tara's eyebrows snapped together at the mention of the doctor again. "Exactly. So my daughter needs to help *herself* and not get worked up about me. Got it? You have your own life and your own dreams, Nikki. And they don't include moonlighting as a—an exotic dancer, for goodness' sake!"

"Fine. Great. Sorry, I had to pay my credit card bill—and someone else already invented the computer and nobody's offered me a job on Wall Street with a gazillion-dollar, tax-payer-funded bonus."

"Don't change the subject."

Like you just did? But Nikki didn't say it aloud.

"Honey, my issues, whether health or financial, are

not your problem. Why do you always feel as if they are?"

"You're my mom."

"Yes?" Tara looked at her strangely. "And you're young and should be enjoying yourself."

Nikki hunched her shoulders.

"What? What is it?"

"Mom…you had me when you were younger than I am right now. You could have— I mean, you had another choice, all right? But you had me and you raised me, even though I'm sure I was a huge burden, and I—"

Tara's eyes widened. "You were never a burden!"

"I guess I just want to, I don't know…be worth it. Make you proud. Pay you back or something."

Her mother's jaw dropped. "Nicole Roslyn Fine, that is the sweetest, most erroneous, *idiotic* and frankly *disturbing* thing I've ever heard."

She marched over and took Nikki by the shoulders. "Stop it. Stop thinking that way this instant, do you hear me? You were a gift, a beautiful gift, and never a cross to bear. Understand?" She shook Nikki. *"Do you understand?"*

"Mom, don't get all upset—"

"I will get upset, young lady. You do not have to prove yourself worthy of my love. And I *am* proud of you, every single day. You have been the very best thing in my life, made me the happiest, and I've never once questioned my decision to bring you into this world. So I don't want to hear another word about being worthy or paying me back, for Lord's sake. You pay me back every day just by being you."

Tears sprang to Nikki's eyes as Tara hugged her fiercely, and she hugged her back, inhaling the scents of cinnamon, vanilla extract, butter and flour that clung to her mom's hair—and had as long as she could remember.

"I love you," Tara said. "And I'll love you whether you get photographed wearing red butt-floss and pasties, or whether you get filmed blowing the president under his desk—"

"Mom!"

"Not that I'd encourage you to do that," Tara said hastily.

"I love you, too," Nikki said around both the shocked laughter and the lump in her throat.

"Good. Now that we have that cleared up, focus on your own problems, not mine. Okay?"

Nikki reluctantly nodded.

Tara sighed, wiped her own eyes and walked to the bakery's front door, where she glanced at her watch, then flipped the sign from Closed to Open, and unlocked the bolt.

"Seven o'clock," she said. "Time to sell the doughnuts." She shot Nikki a look of maternal tolerance. "And really, honeybun. Have a little faith."

Huh. As soon as she was sure she wouldn't cry into the muffin batter, Nikki began spooning it into paper muffin cups while Tara checked on the coffee in preparation for the morning rush. She'd gone to the back room to put on the music when the door chimes rang, signaling that a customer had come in.

Nikki wiped her hands and went to wait on the person. He was tall and about her age, and something about his face and his bowlegged stance was familiar. He had sandy, curly hair and a very ruddy complexion, as if he worked outdoors all day.

"Hi," he said. "I'm Gib Tanner. Is Mrs. Fine here?"

"Just a moment," said Nikki. "I'll get her."

As she went to get her mother, she realized where she'd seen the guy before—at that awful bachelor party. She hunched her shoulders and thanked heaven that she was wearing her hair tied back and no makeup. He didn't seem to have recognized her. Why was he here? Was it an unfortunate coincidence?

"Mom. Someone to see you," she called.

Tara went up front. Since the music was now on, Nikki couldn't hear exactly what was said, but she did catch the words *roof* and *crew* and *Saturday.* What was going on?

Then the door chimes tinkled again and her mother appeared in the kitchen looking dazed.

"What was that about?" Nikki asked.

"That boy, Gib Tanner? He's coming with a crew to work on my roof next Saturday."

"Say what?"

Tara nodded. "That's exactly what he said."

"Huh? Who recommended him? What's his estimate? And how are you going to pay him?"

Tara shook her head. "There's no estimate. No bill. He said a friend of yours sent him, a fraternity brother of his, and not to worry about anything. He'd get me all fixed up."

"What?"

"He has a construction company, he says. Him and his dad."

"They're doing this *free?*"

"Well…I guess so. He said all he needed was permission to go on the property."

"Wait a minute. This is crazy, Mom. Stuff like this doesn't happen."

"Apparently it does." Tara still looked dazed, but she glanced heavenward and her lips moved.

"Is this Gib person licensed? Insured? Bonded?"

"He showed me a bunch of papers to do with that."

"Were they real?"

"Nikki!"

"Well? Seriously. And who is this supposed friend of mine?" Nikki found herself getting more and more agitated. The Gib guy had been at the bachelor party, no doubt about it. "What's the name of my *friend?*"

"Adam, he said."

"Adam?" Nikki choked. "Adam's a jerk and he doesn't have any money."

"Who is Adam?"

"A jerk, like I said." Nikki's head spun.

"He can't be too much of a jerk if he's doing this, sweetie."

Nikki growled something about ulterior motives and stomped out of the kitchen. Should she call him? What *was* his motive? How could he be paying for this? Or did the Gib guy owe him a favor? If so, it had to be one serious favor—like hiding a body or something.

Hadn't there been some mob-run construction company in the news recently when a bunch of corpses were found under a parking garage?

Right. And Gib looked so very Italian...not. What did she think, that the name *Tanner* was Sicilian?

Well, but it could have been shortened at Ellis Island from, um, Tanzale or Tantofino or Tiramisu.

Okay, she was an idiot. Gib looked as Scots/Irish as it was possible to get, and Tanner was most likely English in origin.

She was *so* confused. She would not call Adam. He was the reason she'd gotten fired. But—

Why had he done this?

This was way too elaborate for an apology. This was rooted in something else. But what?

Nikki grabbed her cell phone and dialed half his number before snapping the phone closed. Then she dropped it into her pocket and went back to portioning out the muffin batter.

She refused to make contact with him. And if he so much as polluted the screen of her phone with his number, she'd bake it along with the muffins.

21

ADAM STOOD IN THE MEN'S room and splashed cold water on his face repeatedly before drying off with a paper towel, replacing his glasses and steeling himself for the hour ahead. He and Dev had an appointment to see Dean Trammel. Goal: the reinstatement of Nikki's job.

He straightened his collar and lapels in the mirror and practiced his most winning sixteen-tooth smile, which would do absolutely no good if Dev didn't give the performance of his life and flash his *eighteen*-tooth smile, in which the corners of his mouth almost nudged his ears.

Adam had made Dev rehearse his role of graphic designer over and over, and one of Hal Underwood's employees had provided him with an entire portfolio of his work, plus the fake originals of a different girl's head on Nikki's body and a different guy's head on Adam's.

Dev, who stood at the urinals behind him, finished his whiz biz and zipped up. Then he came to wash his hands.

"You ready to rock, Mr. Photoshop?" Adam asked him.

Dev cracked his neck and eyed his preppy new look in the mirror with disgust. "Yeah. I want to get this over with before my balls turn tartan and my 'Vette morphs into a Volvo."

Adam rolled his eyes. "Remember, the tall bony crone is Margaret, and she's in charge of the Perez scholarship stuff. Work your magic on her. Tell her you hear she makes the best cheesecake in the country— lie and say I gave you a piece. Make her feel like Miss America."

"Done. Women love me—you know that."

"One of life's great unsolved mysteries," Adam muttered. "Come on. We need to get in there."

He took a deep breath and exhaled slowly as they left the men's room and marched down the hallway to the dean's office.

Inside, Margaret sat at the reception desk in Nikki's absence, looking none too happy about it.

"Hi," Adam said cautiously.

"You," she said, dismissing him with a flicker of her eyes.

"Er, yes. It's me, Adam Burke. And this is my friend Devon McKee. We have a two-o'clock appointment with the dean."

Dev shot her the eighteen-tooth grin that he'd perfected on so many women over the years. "Are you the culinary genius who makes that legendary cheesecake?"

"Don't try to butter me up," she snapped.

"Oh, no, ma'am. I'm serious as a heart attack. I dream about that cake." Dev's voice had dropped half an octave, into his signature nightclub croon. "Adam gave me a piece."

Margaret looked up and scanned Dev from head to toe while he made eyes at her, too. Dev had an enviable trick of seeming to stroke a woman with his gaze, lingering just a flattering touch too long on her best features, and then coming to rest at her eyes again, where he deepened his smile suggestively and quirked his lips.

It was masterful, if nauseating to watch.

"Mmm," Dev said, leaving it open to interpretation whether he meant Margaret or the cake.

Too much, Adam thought, but before his eyes Maggie actually fluttered her sparse eyelashes.

Dev leaned forward, not enough to be completely obvious, but enough to suggest conspiracy. "I don't suppose you'd share the recipe, would you?"

Margaret's color heightened; her cheeks flushed a delicate rose. "It's a family thing. We keep it close to the vest."

Dev gazed into her raisinlike eyes for a beat too long before he averted them. "Lucky vest," he murmured.

Adam swallowed a snort. *No, he did* not *just say that.*

Margaret's mouth opened slightly and she put her hands up to her cheeks. Then she shook a finger at him.

Dev leaned in a couple more inches. "You sure I can't talk you out of it, hmm? It was the sweetest thing…all creamy and delicious." His grin had widened until Adam could swear that twenty teeth were showing. All very white and professionally sincere.

"You," she said, shaking her head but dimpling.

It was the polar opposite of the *you* she'd addressed to Adam when they came in.

"You're a naughty boy," Margaret said.

Adam prayed she wouldn't offer to spank Dev right there and then.

"No, ma'am," Dev said. "I'm good. Good through and through." He winked a bordello-blue eye. "Just like your tasty cake."

Under Adam's disbelieving eyes, Margaret giggled.

And just as he thought he'd hurl on his shoes, the door to the dean's office opened; the man emerged.

"Sir," Margaret said, "these two young men are here to see you."

Adam smiled and stuck out his hand. "Yes, sir, we are." He introduced himself and then Dev, and they followed Dean Trammel into his office, where he told them to take a seat.

"How can I help you two?" the dean asked.

"Well, sir, we're here to clear up a misunderstanding," Adam said. "Two days ago, as you may remember, some racy pictures were tacked to the bulletin board in the hall."

Dean Trammel's eyes flashed with sudden recognition. "You were the boy in the pictures," he said, frowning.

"Well, sir, it did look that way."

Trammel raised his eyebrows. "You're going to tell me that you have an evil twin? Come on, Mr. Burke. Pictures don't lie."

"Excuse me, sir," Dev said smoothly, "but there are times when they do."

Trammel crossed his arms across his chest and leaned back, his body language stating clearly, *Oh, I can't wait to hear this one.*

"You may have heard of Photoshop, sir?"

The dean nodded curtly.

"As a graphic designer I use it every day. And as an old fraternity brother of Adam's, here, I used it to play a tasteless joke on him."

"Go on."

"Adam, see, is all work and no play. He studies constantly, sir, and any muscles he has are purely from hefting those fifty-pound medical texts of his."

Adam cut his eyes at Dev. *Don't lay it on too thick.*

"Well, anyway, a very good friend of ours got married last weekend, and Burke, here, refused even to go to the bachelor party because he had too much studying to do. We weren't happy about that. So early this week, we decided to punk him."

"Punk?"

"Er, play a prank on him. And see, I knew that he had this instant crush on a girl who worked here in your office. So, sir, I got a couple of shots of her while she was walking on campus, and I used Photoshop to put her head onto the body of the stripper from the bachelor party. Then I did the same thing with Adam's head and the, um, bachelor's body."

"That's possible?"

"Yes. I can show you the original photos if you'd like." Dev patted the zipped black portfolio he'd brought with him.

"That won't be necessary," the dean said. Then, "You pinned them to the bulletin board as a joke?"

"Yes, sir." Dev made a good show of looking shamefaced. "I didn't think about the consequences, sir."

"No, you did not," Trammel said scathingly. "I fired the poor girl."

Dev nodded unhappily. "That's what I understand. I'm here, Dean Trammel, to ask you to reconsider. Because my actions harmed her unfairly—and harmed my friend Adam, as well. They are innocent parties in all of this, and I can't tell you how sorry I am."

Dean Trammel looked him over in silence. Then he looked at Adam, who met his gaze squarely. Trammel transferred his gaze back to Dev and blew out a disgusted breath. "Why don't you try."

"Excuse me, sir?"

"Try. Telling me—and Mr. Burke—how sorry you are."

"Ah. Yes." Dev swallowed. "I apologize from the bottom of my heart, sir. I really do." He turned to Adam. "I'm sorry I was a dirtbag."

"And a scum-sucking bottom-feeder," Adam couldn't help adding. "And a degenerate pig."

Trammel's lips twitched.

They waited for several beats in silence before the dean got up and rounded his desk, their cue to get up, as well.

"Mr. Burke, I'm sorry that I leaped to conclusions. Thank you for being man enough to face me and explain. That can't have been easy. Mr. McKee, I hope you'll think about the possible consequences of your actions in the future. But likewise, thank you for your honesty. While I have no authority over you, since you're not a student here, I would hope that you will also apologize profusely to Nikki Fine."

"Yes, sir. You can be sure of that."

"Excellent." Trammel opened the door and gestured them out. "Gentlemen, have a nice day."

He turned to Margaret as they headed for the reception exit. "Will you get Nikki Fine on the phone for me? Thank you."

NIKKI CURLED INTO a fetal position after work, her feet throbbing from standing all day at the bakery. She closed her eyes and ignored the blinking red light on the phone that told her insistently that she had voice mail.

Anyone she cared about talking to had her cell phone number. That meant the message was a hang-up from a telemarketer or a political action committee, or a representative from her college or a charity asking for money that she didn't have.

She closed her eyes against the insistent little red light and gave a weary yawn. She was hungry, having avoided chowing down countless pastries and muffins at Sweetheart's, but she was too tired and too demoralized to get up and make herself something to eat.

She wanted to fall asleep and wake up again with feet that didn't throb. But her T-shirt had absorbed the aromas of the bakery, and so every breath she took reminded her of how hungry she was.

A nice big greasy pepperoni pizza would do the trick. She had a twenty-dollar bill in her sock drawer... but then she'd have to sit up and find the number of the pizza place. She'd have to expend energy she didn't have by dialing the phone and actually speaking to someone, and she'd been smiling at and speaking to strangers all day, making change and filling little paper bags with muffins and Danishes and doughnuts.

Maybe if she prayed for a pizza it would show up, like her mom's gift roofers. Okay, that was a bit sacrilegious, so she apologized to God.

No sooner had she done so than a knock sounded on her door.

Nikki sat up, rubbing her eyes. Maybe God *had* sent a pizza. No, she was kidding herself.

The knock sounded again. Nikki heaved her legs over the side of the bed and stood, then ambled to the door in her bare feet. She peered out the keyhole to see Adam and another guy standing there.

22

Nikki groaned at the sight of the two jerks.

No. She was not opening the door. Absolutely not.

She smelled like a giant cookie, she had no makeup on, and she hated both of them. Therefore, she was not home.

"Nikki?" Adam called. "I know you're in there. Your car is in the lot."

So? She could be at a neighbor's. She could be in the shower. She could be walking her invisible dog.

Nikki said nothing.

Then the other guy, who must be the idiot Dev, put his eye to the peephole to try to see in. *My kingdom for a sharp stick.* Really, did she have a pencil handy? She could jab it right into his eye through the hole.

"Nikki?" Adam called again. "Please. Just give us a moment of your time. We want to apologize."

And a fat lot of good that would do. Would it get her job back? Would it erase the public humiliation of having the dean and Margaret see her practically naked? She thought not.

Nikki turned her back on the door and walked to

her bedroom again. She crawled under the covers and began thinking about food. Burgers with bacon and cheese. Crispy egg rolls and pork fried rice. A giant deep-dish pizza with extra pepperoni. Her stomach gave a last, anguished growl before she drifted into dreamland, where she sat at a red-gingham-covered table and ate them all.

She woke disoriented a couple of hours later, unsure of what had brought her to consciousness. Then she realized what it was—another knock on the door. Why was her apartment Grand Central Station today? Annoyed, she rolled out of bed and stumbled to the peephole for the second time.

A fast-food delivery man stood outside. With a pizza! Nikki's stomach practically yodeled in gastric delight. God *had* sent her a pizza, despite her doubt and disrespect a couple of hours ago.

She'd unlocked the door and opened it before she thought about how weird and coincidental this was. And so when the delivery man turned and she saw that it was the Dev guy under the red-and-blue cap, it was too late. He stuck his foot inside in case she tried to slam the door on him, then kissed her cheek and said, "Hey, babe!" before she could even hiss.

Adam appeared behind him with, of all things, a portable CD player. "Nikki," he said, "meet Dev. Dev, Nikki."

Looking faintly apologetic, he pressed Play, and pulsing, throbbing stripper music boomed out.

Dev's hips began to gyrate before Nikki could close her gaping mouth and scream, "No!"

He flashed her a diabolical, dazzling grin and cakewalked into the apartment, doing his best Michael Jackson impersonation while she backed away from him.

Pizza box balanced on his upturned palm, Dev then whirled and gave her the back view, shaking his butt and grooving with his pelvis. He smoothed his free hand over one bun in a laughably perverted way, trailing it down his thigh before spinning again to face her.

Two things prevented her from diving for the phone and calling 911. First, she couldn't help laughing at the idiot. And second, the pizza was *real*. The scents of pepperoni, cheese, onion and garlic wafted out of the box, infinitely more seductive than doofus Dev and his pathetic crotch-grabbing antics.

Damn it, she was *mad* at them. She didn't *want* to laugh! It made her even madder, which made her laugh harder, which made it very difficult to stay angry. And the two guys knew it, which gave her the urge to slam both of their heads together.

This was manipulation, plain and simple.

Over the music and her own laughter, she heard the unmistakable sound of Velcro being peeled, and suddenly Dev's pizza-man shirt went flying past her. He dropped the pizza box on her coffee table and laced his fingers behind his neck, thrusting his own, er… pepperoni forward shamelessly in time to the music.

She averted her gaze to Adam's face. He looked pained.

In Dev's defense, he had a very nice chest and a flat, muscular tummy. But Nikki lunged for the pizza and ignored him, while Adam turned off the soundtrack.

"Okay, that's enough, stripper-boy," he said.

Dev stopped dancing, looking a little sheepish. "Aw, man. I didn't even get to rip off my pants."

"And I'm deeply thankful for that," said Adam fervently.

Nikki opened the box and inhaled with appreciation. "You two," she said, taking a slice, "are beyond pathetic."

"We know," Adam agreed. "But we really are desperate to apologize."

Nikki raised her eyebrows, unable to say anything because her mouth was full of divine carbohydrates and salt and grease. She chewed and swallowed, having only one thing to say before she took a second bite. "Go ahead."

"Right. We'll do that. But Dev wants to put his shirt back on first, don't you, Dev?"

"I do?"

"Yes. Would you want *your* girlfriend ogling *my* naked chest?"

"I don't have a girlfriend," Dev pointed out.

"That is beside the point—"

"Neither do you, Adam," Nikki said acidly.

Adam nodded. "Fair enough. But I hope to, er, change that in the next few minutes."

"Really?" she said, around another bite of pizza. "How interesting."

"Dev is going to apologize first," Adam said. "Aren't you, Dev? Then he's going to go."

"Mmm," Nikki replied. "Well, if he's your ride, then I hope he doesn't go far."

Adam sighed. "Dev?"

Devon haphazardly stuck his shirt back together and then slid to his knees in front of Nikki as if she were first base. "Babe," he began.

She shook her head. "Not acceptable."

"Doll?" asked Dev.

"Nope."

"Queen Nikki?"

"Better." She pulled a piece of melted cheese off her next slice and dripped it into her mouth.

"Okay. Queen Nikki, I most humbly and excruciatingly apologize for my dastardly, bastardly behavior. I hope that you can forgive me."

She rolled her eyes. "Why don't you say this like you actually mean it?"

Dev nodded. "'Kay. Nikki, in all seriousness, I was a toxic, half-drunk asshole when I put up those pictures. I was trying to punk him. I didn't think about the consequences to you, or to Adam. I'm really, really sorry."

"Wow," Nikki said in wondering tones. "I think you may not be acting."

"I'm not acting, Nikki. And in fact, Adam and I went to see—"

"I'll do that part, Dev. Thanks," Adam said firmly. He stood up. "I'd like to be alone with Nikki now."

"If that's okay with her," Nikki interjected. "After all, this is *her* apartment that you've invaded. You might want to ask."

Adam took a deep breath and turned to face her. "Is it okay?"

She put the pizza down and wiped her hands on a tissue from the box on her coffee table. She shrugged, then nodded grudgingly.

Dev got to his feet and turned the silly cap around on his head so that the visor of it hung over his neck. He shoved his hands into his pockets. "Nikki, I truly am sorry. And you can be sure that whatever I have to do to fix it, I will do. Okay?"

"I don't think it's fixable, Dev." Her voice was quiet. "But I do appreciate your apology."

He nodded and walked to the door.

"Even if you got in here by playing yet another trick on me," she tossed after him.

Dev, his hand on the doorknob, looked over his shoulder and gave her a rueful wink. Then he left.

ADAM SAT NEXT TO Nikki on the couch. She'd never looked more beautiful to him than right now, in her torn jeans and mussed ponytail, still with sheet marks on her face. She had a pizza crumb lurking in the left corner of her mouth, where she got a dimple when she smiled.

She wasn't smiling right now.

Acid churned through his stomach and took a running leap for his throat, but he swallowed and ignored it. "Nikki, we went and talked to the dean today."

She stared at him. "And said what?"

"I made Dev tell him that he put your face and my face onto different bodies with Photoshop."

Adam didn't like the silence that ensued.

"So you lied," she finally said.

Adam didn't know how he'd expected her to react, but it wasn't with this cool disdain. "Yes, we lied. But—"

"Why?"

He stared at her. "To smooth everything over. To get your job back for you."

"You asked him to reinstate me?" Shock registered on her face.

Adam nodded. "He asked Margaret to get you on the phone before we'd even left the office."

Nikki looked over at her answering machine, which

was blinking. "That's who the message is from, then," she murmured.

Adam nodded. "Yes, probably. He thanked us for coming to talk to him face-to-face, and he was upset that he'd fired you unjustly."

Nikki balled up the tissue in her hand and tucked her feet up under her on the sofa. "But he didn't fire me unjustly," she said. "That was *me* up there on the bulletin board in the G-string."

"Well, yes, but—"

"Regardless of how the pictures got up there, it was my unfortunate choice to dress like that, and Dean Trammel was within his rights to react the way he did."

"Okay." Adam sucked in his cheeks, perplexed.

"Also, did you bother to ask me whether I wanted to work there, before you pulled this stunt?"

Uh-oh.

"It never occurred to me that you wouldn't want your job back," he said. "So no, I didn't talk to you first—not that you would have let me, anyway."

"I feel like a puppet."

"What? Why?"

"And you're pulling my strings, mine and the dean's…"

"No," he said hotly. "I'm trying to make things right, damn it!"

The words rang between them.

After a moment she sighed and reached out to touch his arm. "I know that. And I know that you're sorry for what happened. But I'm overwhelmed right now and I feel upside down and inside out. And bringing me a pizza and a pack of well-intentioned lies can't fix what's broken."

He could think of absolutely nothing to say. Finally he dredged up a question. "Did Gib stop by your mother's bakery?"

Nikki nodded, and pursed her lips. "That's another thing. I know you're responsible for that, and there's a part of me that wants to hug you and kiss you and fall in love with you because of it...."

Hey, sounded good to him.

"But there's another part of me that says, whoa! Don't fix my mom's roof out of guilt. And that I don't want to be beholden to you and what are you going to want in return?"

Anger kindled within him. "Now you're being flat-out insulting. I don't want anything in return. And I didn't talk to Gib out of guilt. I spoke with him days ago, after you confided in me. And I did it simply because he knows all too well how hard single mothers have it—his aunt Randi is a single mom.

"If it's any consolation to you, we fixed her roof and built her a screen porch, too. Gib and his dad and I worked with all of our fraternity brothers to do it— which, incidentally, is where the labor will come from next Saturday. Everyone's taking the day to help."

He folded his arms across his chest and glared at her. "And just to set your mind at ease, none of the guys showed up at Gib's aunt's expecting to be *serviced.* None of them have asked for more than a glass of ice water in return."

Nikki reddened under his gaze. Good. She deserved to squirm. "I'm sorry," she said. "I was out of line."

"Damn right you were."

"But why are you doing this? You don't even *know* my mom."

Adam pinched the bridge of his nose between his

thumb and forefinger. How had solving Nikki's problems become another problem? He didn't understand.

"I know *you*," he said. "And that's good enough for me. I'm a guy. We like to fix things, especially for the women in our lives. It makes us feel useful. You could even say that it's the way we express our love. Okay?"

Nikki's gaze snapped to his. "What did you say?" she whispered.

He returned her gaze. "You heard me," he said evenly. "Look, Nikki, I'm not going to propose marriage after knowing you for a week, but I have a feeling about us."

Her mouth opened but no sound came out.

He took advantage of that and kissed her, thoroughly. The way she opened to him and melted beneath his mouth told him what he needed to know. "You don't have to say anything in response, okay? I know your emotions are all over the place right now. But please, accept my apology and let me at least get that friggin' roof done."

He got up, closed the lid of the pizza box and cupped her chin in his hand. Then he dropped a kiss on top of her curly, blond head and made his exit while she stared after him, still mute.

23

NIKKI OPENED THE BAKERY by herself on Saturday, since her mother wanted to be home when the guys showed up to work on her roof.

She had listened to the message from Dean Trammel, which was polite and to the point. He apologized for jumping to conclusions and said that she was welcome back in his office. She'd called him, thanked him and asked for a few days to think things over.

Because, as she'd told Adam, she didn't know how she felt about returning to work there. She'd been dismissed in disgrace and she was sure the reason for her firing had run like wildfire through the rest of the administrative staff. Did she really want to return and see people's speculative eyes roaming her body?

Besides which, she felt that she'd be going back under false pretenses, since Dev and Adam had lied for her. Were the benefits at the university worth it? Did she really want the job, or had she angled for it simply because she wanted the health insurance?

That was a tough one. Nikki certainly couldn't say that she lived to file papers or to type letters or to deal with office mates like Margaret. But besides being committed to paying off her medical debt…what exactly did she live for?

You have your own life and your own dreams, Nikki.

Her mother had said that to her. Was she avoiding having to deal with her own future by worrying about her mother?

Of course not.

Well, maybe.

Oh, boy, was this hard to admit.

Yes.

So then what *were* her dreams, exactly?

Panic kicked in. She didn't know. She was twenty-four years old, with a degree in business administration, and she had no clue what she wanted out of life, besides a family and her own business in *something.* Something that had to do with helping single moms.

And that was scary, because two-thirds of all new businesses failed within the first two years they were in operation.

And there, in that statement, lay her problem: fear. Nikki groaned.

It was a little demoralizing to find out that the mother she'd enjoyed patronizing about sticking her head in the sand was, in fact, braver than she was.

Tara had started her own business without a college degree, and she'd done it with a toddler for a partner.

Nikki started the morning coffee for Sweetheart's huge urns and then began mixing a bowl of batter for blueberry scones. Maybe, just maybe, Dev and Adam had done her a favor by getting her fired. Thanks to Adam, she now had a choice again and she could make it clear-eyed: go back to the safety of doing boring work for the university, or strike out on her own.

There were loans available for women who started businesses. And yes, she could probably even cover major medical insurance out of such a business loan. She *could* cut her costs by moving in with her mother, just as Tara had lived with her parents when she'd started the bakery.

As for the cats peeing and digging in the plants, what if they designated one room as the garden room and moved all the plants in there?

One by one the pieces fell into place as Nikki mixed and baked and waited on customers. By the end of the day, when she flipped the sign on the door to Closed and locked the place up, she'd figured out everything except the particulars of what training programs her business was going to offer single moms, and what government subsidies might be available to help her help them. That would require some research.

She climbed into her car in a cloud of cinnamon, walnuts and vanilla and drove to her mother's house, wondering if Adam and the guys would still be there. It was only a little after six when she pulled up outside, and sure enough, the roof was dotted with hot, sweaty, young torsos.

It was quite a sight, all that testosterone gleaming up there in the sun. Nikki shaded her eyes and looked for one chest in particular: Adam's. And there he was, grinning at her, his thumbs hooked through the belt-loops of his snug, faded jeans.

That was no six-pack riding above his leather tool belt. It was more of an eight-pack. His chest and arms rippled with muscle. The guy might wear glasses, but he was no geek.

"Hi," he said, pushing the glasses up to the bridge

of his nose. "Is it warm out here, or is it you steaming up my lenses?"

She looked down at her batter-speckled T-shirt and the coffee stain on her thigh. "It's all me," she said dryly.

"I don't suppose you two have any more cold water in the house?"

"It's a good possibility. Would you like me to get you some?"

"Please."

She nodded and went in the front door. "Mom?"

Tara didn't answer, but her old Corolla was in the driveway.

"Mom?" Nikki heard a strange, faint noise from the kitchen and started running, past the burgundy wing chairs and the antique tea table and over the oriental rug that had been in the house for as long as she could remember. A cat meowed in the kitchen, followed by a human moan.

Nikki burst into the kitchen to find Tara lying on the floor, looking dazed. "Mom! Mom, what happened? Are you okay? Oh, my God," she babbled, as she dropped to her knees beside her. The refrigerator door was wide open, and a chair lay overturned.

Tara struggled up to a sitting position, wincing in pain, and touched the back of her skull gingerly. "I think I hit my head."

"How? Did you fall?"

Her mother nodded. "I—I got real dizzy again, honeybun, and I grabbed for the fridge door, but it opened and I went backward."

"Oh, my God." As frustration with her mother's refusal to get checked by a doctor warred with love and concern, Nikki noticed that her mother's pupils were larger than usual. "I don't think you should move, okay?"

"Well, of course I'm going to move, Nicole. I can't sit on the kitchen floor all day." But when Tara tried to get to her feet, she wobbled. "Lord, am I dizzy."

"Let me take your weight," Nikki ordered. "Come on—we're going to the sofa." She half dragged her mother to the couch in the living room and settled her on it. "I'm going to call an ambulance."

"No, sweetheart, you're not. They called one for Mrs. Sorkin down the street when she fell, and she got a fifteen-hundred-dollar bill for a two-mile ride."

"I don't care. You need to go to the emergency room—"

"Forget it. This is a bump on the head, that's all."

"But you got dizzy enough this time that you fell. You fainted, Mom. You could have a—" She stopped herself from saying *brain tumor* just in time.

"Get me some ice, honey. Stop making a big deal out of this."

"It *is* a big deal." Nikki ran to the kitchen and filled a plastic bag with ice cubes, then wrapped it in a dish towel. She took it to her mother and then ran for the door.

"Where are you going?"

"Adam!" Nikki called. "Adam, please. I need your help down here. My mother fell and hit her head."

In moments he was on the ground and hurrying toward her. "What happened?"

"I don't know. She gets these dizzy spells. And this time she fell backward. She hit her head on the floor."

"She's conscious?"

"Yes."

"Okay, calm down. Let me take a look at her." Adam

touched her reassuringly on the shoulder, then apparently got a whiff of himself. He smelled pretty ripe, but so would any guy who'd been working on a roof all day.

Nikki took him inside and introduced him to her mother. "Mom, this is my friend Adam. He's—"

"Dear Lord!" Her mother fanned herself with a magazine after getting a good look at Adam's sweaty, bronzed chest and tool belt. "I think I'm going to faint *again.*"

"Mrs. Fine, I'm not a doctor, but—"

"You did stay at a Holiday Inn last night?" Tara said, a tongue-in-cheek reference to the hotel chain's ads.

"He's in medical school," Nikki broke in.

Tara stopped fanning herself and glowered at him.

"I'd like to ask you some questions, if you don't mind." Adam knelt beside her and put two fingers to the inside of her wrist.

"You're training to become a quack?"

"Mom!"

Adam looked taken aback but laughed. "Well, for a lady who just took a big fall, you sure are a firecracker."

"I don't believe in doctors."

"Mom, *stop it,*" said Nikki.

Adam's eyebrows rose. "Well, it's a good thing that I'm not one, then, isn't it?"

Tara eyed him suspiciously, but then her gaze fell to his nude, sweaty chest again, distracting her from his evil future profession.

He took full advantage of this. "So what happened, exactly?"

"I got very dizzy," Tara told him, "and tried to grab on to something but lost my balance and fell."

"Did you have a headache?"

"Not really. I do now," she said ruefully, rubbing at the back of her head.

"Look into my eyes for a moment, okay?"

"If you insist," said Tara, "but quite honestly I'd rather look at your chest." She shot a mischievous glance at Nikki.

Adam reddened a little, but he took it in stride. "Hmm. Your pupils are a little enlarged."

"What does that mean?"

"Well, this is only a quack theory, you understand—" Adam's eyes twinkled "—but it *could* be a sign of concussion. Mrs. Fine, are you having any double vision or blurriness in your eyes?"

She shook her head.

"Okay. What about chest pain, difficulty breathing, leg or arm weakness?"

Again she shook her head to each question.

"Good." Adam placed his palm on her forehead. "I don't think you have a fever...but I don't like the dizziness, the fall or your enlarged pupils. I'd suggest that we get you to the nearest E.R. and have a real doctor take a look at you."

"No, no, that won't be necessary," said Tara.

"Yes, it will," Nikki told her.

Tara glared at her. "You know how I feel about the Western medical/pharmaceutical racket. And even if I believed in it, I don't have the cash—"

Adam once again manfully ignored the insult and focused on the real problem. "Do you have medical insurance, Mrs. Fine?"

"No," Nikki said baldly. "She doesn't. It's an issue."

Adam looked from her to Tara and back again. "Okay. Hang on a sec." He dug into his pocket for his phone, pulled it out and stepped into the next room. Nikki heard him speak in a low voice to someone, his tone concerned. He repeated her mother's symptoms. "All right, thank you. Thanks very much. We'll come right over."

He came back into the living room. "I've arranged for you to see an instructor of mine. He's going to meet us at his office. He's an ENT guy."

"Another quack," moaned Tara.

"No, Mrs. Fine," Adam said firmly. "He's very good."

"ENT?" asked Nikki.

"Ear, nose and throat doctor. Your inner ears have a lot to do with your sense of balance, Mrs. Fine. So he'll be able to test you to see if what you're experiencing is a little bit of BPPV or something else. He'll also do a scan to make sure you don't have a severe concussion. Okay?"

"BPPV?" To Nikki's relief, Tara seemed to have responded unconsciously to the note of authority in Adam's voice.

"Benign Paroxysmal Positional Vertigo," Adam explained. "Quite common, actually."

"But—"

"There won't be any charge. Look at it this way— he's a teacher, I'm a student. You're my very own quack case study. How about that?"

Reluctantly, Tara smiled at him. Then she nodded.

Nikki lost her own balance at that moment. Because she fell hopelessly, irretrievably in love with Adam Burke right then and there, with no reservations at all.

Forget Aunt Dee's experience and clichés about starter wives. *I'm going to marry him,* Nikki thought. *Even if, God forbid, Dev is his best man.*

24

ADAM AND NIKKI WAITED outside the examination room as Adam's instructor, the ENT doc, took a look at her mother. Nikki paced back and forth, clearly worried. Even in her oversize T-shirt, jeans, old shoes and batter smears, Adam thought again how beautiful she was.

Women seemed to think they looked their best in full makeup and a fancy outfit, but he disagreed. This Nikki was the real one, the tangible one—as opposed to the fantasy girl who'd jumped out of the cake at Mark's bachelor party.

"Nikki," Adam said. He crossed the room and took her hand. "It's going to be okay."

She looked up at him, her face pale, her mouth working. She'd chewed a spot on her lip until it had turned angry and swollen, and now she couldn't stop touching it.

He reached out a finger and ran it gently over the tiny wound. "Hey, stop that. I have a vested interest in keeping your mouth intact."

That won him the ghost of a smile. "Oh, yeah? And what would that be?"

"Well," Adam murmured, pulling her closer, "I like to kiss it." And he did, cupping her face in his hands and doing his best to communicate, wordlessly, how he felt about her.

She broke the kiss first. "Thank you for being so understanding and sweet with my mom. She's not crazy about doctors, as you may have guessed by now."

He shrugged and chuckled. "It's actually a refreshing change to have a girl's mother disapprove of my chosen profession."

"Oh, most of them start planning the wedding immediately, huh?"

"Something like that."

"Well, you definitely won't have that problem with my mom. Not only doesn't she like doctors, but she isn't sold on the whole concept of marriage, either. She feels that she's done pretty well raising me on my own."

"I'd have to agree," Adam said lightly.

"And her sister was married to an orthopedic surgeon, until he dumped her—after she'd helped to pay off all his school loans and had his children."

"That explains a lot. So I'm literally Dr. Evil to her?"

"You handled her beautifully," Nikki said, the little diplomat.

"Listen." Adam drew her to a seating area in the corner. "I want to talk to you about something you said to me."

"Uh-oh." Nikki sat gingerly on the edge of a chair. "Something I said when I was mad?"

"Yes. But I deserved it. And I want to explain. You accused me of blowing hot and cold—and I can see how you might have thought that. But I never meant to be cold to you. I guess I just felt that I had to compensate for being so distracted by you. I'd spend time with you and then panic because I had to catch up on studying. I'm very disciplined, but I'm afraid that if I slip up then it'll create a domino effect—a disaster."

"Why does it have to be so all or nothing, Adam?"

"That's what I'm trying to explain. See, I haven't always been a great student. I screwed up big-time in high school when I fell for a girl and got so wrapped up in her—and partying with her—that I let my grades go. Then I couldn't get into any of the colleges that had pre-med programs."

He sighed. "I ended up hating her for it, and that wasn't fair. *I* made the choices that I did, not her. *I* messed up my plans for my future."

Nikki nodded. "But it's true that she distracted you."

Adam ran a hand over the back of his neck. "What seventeen-year-old kid isn't sidetracked by his first sexual relationship? You think you're in love. You think nothing else could possibly matter."

Nikki's mouth curved in understanding, possibly memories of her own first love. He found himself fiercely jealous of the unknown boy and pushed away the emotion.

"Anyway. Once I figured out that the sun and the stars didn't revolve around that girl or my dick, I had to work my butt off in junior college to even get considered for a transfer to a four-year school. I had to work even harder—and do extra courses—to get admitted to the pre-med program. And I swore that I would never screw up my life for a girl again, because I won't get a third chance at med school."

She opened her mouth, but he held up a hand. "Just let me say this, okay? So then, Nikki, I met you. I kept telling myself that I didn't have time for a relationship, a girlfriend. But you weren't just any girl. You were *you.* Impossible to ignore or forget, no matter what."

"You tried to forget me?" Nikki asked in mock outrage.

"Yeah, I did. I'm glad it didn't work, though."

She smiled and kissed him, but he wasn't done talking yet. "Here's the thing, Nikki. I want to see you. I want you to be my girlfriend. But I'm not going to lie—I have very little time and it's not fair to you. You'd probably be happier with a guy who could get away with you on the weekends and have fun—"

Nikki poked him in the chest. "Hold it right there, Doctor Burke. I do believe you're misdiagnosing things."

His eyebrows shot up.

"Don't you think it's up to me to decide who I'm happiest with?"

"Well—"

"And besides, I'll be working a forty- to fifty-hour week, plus researching and writing a business plan on the side. So I may not have as much free time on my hands as you think. Let's put it this way, Adam—I won't be waiting by the phone. You might even have to make an appointment to see me."

He started to laugh. "That's my girl."

"Oh, I'm your girl now, huh?"

Adam sobered in an instant. "Oh, yeah. If you'll have me, Nikki, then you're *definitely* my girl."

NIKKI'S MOTHER WAS DIAGNOSED with a mild concussion and a case of vertigo which had been aggravated by an inner-ear infection. Since she double-checked with a local practitioner of Chinese medicine and he concurred, she was willing to concede that Adam and his instructor were among the more talented "quacks" of Western medicine. Both managed a grave thanks and gladly accepted payment in cheesecake and other pastries.

Gib and the rest of the boys not only fixed Tara's roof, but installed a cat door in the new garden room and cut chicken wire inserts for the indoor planters so that they were no longer attractive feline latrines.

Tara went full-time as a student and gave in, with exasperation, to her daughter's demand that she finally get health insurance through the university.

Adam ended up a finalist for the Perez scholarship, but was not the final winner. He applied for four others.

Dev and Adam helped Nikki move in to her mother's house and she took over at Sweetheart's until she could find a buyer for the bakery, half the proceeds of which would go to paying off Nikki's debt. In the meantime she devoted her evenings to researching her future company and writing a business plan. She really *was* almost too busy to see Adam.

Almost.

Tonight, Nikki stood in a trench coat and high heels outside Adam's apartment door. She knocked lightly and waited a few moments before knocking again.

Finally the door opened and Adam stood there, looking bleary-eyed, as if he'd been studying for twelve hours straight.

"Pizza girl," she said, and opened her coat.

His mouth fell open.

"You ordered extra lace on top, right? And a garter belt with stockings?"

He was shirtless and unshaven, just the way she liked him. She placed her palms flat on his chest and pushed him backward, then kicked the door shut behind her and locked it.

"Oh, wow... Nikki, I have an exam tomorrow...."

"And I'm here to relieve all of your tension before it, Doctor Burke." She stripped off the coat and tossed it to the floor. "Besides, what makes you think I'm staying? I have things to do until late...and I have no intention of getting up at 6:00 a.m., even to ogle your butt as you jog out the door."

"About that," Adam said. "How are we going to handle mornings if we get married?"

"Simple," Nikki told him. "If you insist on being an early-rising alien life-form, then you're going to sneak quietly out of the house and get take-out coffee."

"I am?"

"Yep."

"Well, I'm so glad we got that straightened out."

Nikki grinned, steered him to the couch, pushed him down on it and straddled his lap. She pulled his head forward so that his face rested in her cleavage. "So, do I have to break your nose to get your attention, baby?" she crooned.

Nikki heard the rumble of his laughter deep between her breasts.

"Never again, I swear."

She grabbed the remote control for the TV, which was on the couch beside them, and changed the channel to one with upbeat rock music.

"Now," she said, tilting his chin back up. "Do you want a lap dance, or do you want a *lap* dance?"

Adam was fully awake now. "I'd like both, thanks." He grinned.

"Ooh, I don't know if you have time for that, you

busy boy," she said, trailing her fingers down his chest. "With your big exam and all."

He caught her wrists and held them. "Be nice."

She winked and wiggled on his lap. "But I don't want to be nice. I'm all into the idea of being naughty right now—if, like I said, you have the time."

He drew her toward him and kissed her. "For you, Nikki, I will always make time. Always."

She held his bristly jaw tenderly between her hands. "Shh, don't tell anyone, but I think I love you," she whispered.

"I think I love you, too."

Nikki slid off Adam's knees, hooked a thumb in her G-string and began a very private dance just for him.

This time, he didn't laugh.

* * * * *

PASSION

For a spicier, decidedly hotter read—
this is your destination for romance!

COMING NEXT MONTH
AVAILABLE JANUARY 31, 2012

#663 ONCE UPON A VALENTINE
Bedtime Stories
Stephanie Bond, Leslie Kelly, Michelle Rowen

#664 THE KEEPER
Men Out of Uniform
Rhonda Nelson

#665 CHOOSE ME
It's Trading Men!
Jo Leigh

#666 SEX, LIES AND VALENTINES
Undercover Operatives
Tawny Weber

#667 BRING IT ON
Island Nights
Kira Sinclair

#668 THE PLAYER'S CLUB: LINCOLN
The Player's Club
Cathy Yardley

REQUEST YOUR FREE BOOKS!
2 FREE NOVELS PLUS 2 FREE GIFTS!

red-hot reads!

YES! Please send me 2 FREE Harlequin® Blaze™ novels and my 2 FREE gifts (gifts are worth about $10). After receiving them, if I don't wish to receive any more books, I can return the shipping statement marked "cancel." If I don't cancel, I will receive 6 brand-new novels every month and be billed just $4.49 per book in the U.S. or $4.96 per book in Canada. That's a saving of at least 14% off the cover price. It's quite a bargain. Shipping and handling is just 50¢ per book in the U.S. and 75¢ per book in Canada.* I understand that accepting the 2 free books and gifts places me under no obligation to buy anything. I can always return a shipment and cancel at any time. Even if I never buy another book, the two free books and gifts are mine to keep forever.

151/351 HDN FEQE

Name _____ (PLEASE PRINT) _____

Address _____ Apt. # _____

City _____ State/Prov. _____ Zip/Postal Code _____

Signature (if under 18, a parent or guardian must sign)

Mail to the **Reader Service:**
IN U.S.A.: P.O. Box 1867, Buffalo, NY 14240-1867
IN CANADA: P.O. Box 609, Fort Erie, Ontario L2A 5X3

Not valid for current subscribers to Harlequin Blaze books.

Want to try two free books from another line?
Call 1-800-873-8635 or visit www.ReaderService.com.

HB11B

Rhonda Nelson

SIZZLES WITH ANOTHER INSTALLMENT OF

When former ranger Jack Martin is assigned to provide security to Mariette Levine, a local pastry chef, he believes this will be an open-and-shut case. Yet the danger becomes all too real when Mariette is attacked. But things aren't always what they seem, and soon Jack's protective instincts demand he save the woman he is quickly falling for.

THE KEEPER

**Available February 2012
wherever books are sold.**

HB79668

*Louisa Morgan loves being around children.
So when she has the opportunity to tutor bedridden Ellie,
she's determined to bring joy back into the motherless
girl's world. Can she also help Ellie's father open his
heart again? Read on for a sneak peek of*

THE COWBOY FATHER

*by Linda Ford,
available February 2012 from Love Inspired Historical.*

Why had Louisa thought she could do this job? A bubble of self-pity whispered she was totally useless, but Louisa ignored it. She wasn't useless. She could help Ellie if the child allowed it.

Emmet walked her out, waiting until they were out of earshot to speak. "I sense you and Ellie are not getting along."

"Ellie has lost her freedom. On top of that, everything is new. Familiar things are gone. Her only defense is to exert what little independence she has left. I believe she will soon tire of it and find there are more enjoyable ways to pass the time."

He looked doubtful. Louisa feared he would tell her not to return. But after several seconds' consideration, he sighed heavily. "You're right about one thing. She's lost everything. She can hardly be blamed for feeling out of sorts."

"She hasn't lost everything, though." Her words were quiet, coming from a place full of certainty that Emmet was more than enough for this child. "She has you."

"She'll always have me. As long as I live." He clenched his fists. "And I fully intend to raise her in such a way that even if something happened to me, she would never feel like I was gone. I'd be in her thoughts and in her actions every day."

Peace filled Louisa. "Exactly what my father did."

Their gazes connected, forged a single thought about fathers and daughters…how each needed the other. How sweet the relationship was.

Louisa tipped her head away first. "I'll see you tomorrow."

Emmet nodded. "Until tomorrow then."

She climbed behind the wheel of their automobile and turned toward home. She admired Emmet's devotion to his child. It reminded her of the love her own father had lavished on Louisa and her sisters. Louisa smiled as fond memories of her father filled her thoughts. Ellie was a fortunate child to know such love.

Louisa understands what both father and daughter are going through. Will her compassion help them heal—and form a new family? Find out in
THE COWBOY FATHER
by Linda Ford, available February 14, 2012.

Love Inspired Books celebrates 15 years of inspirational romance in 2012! February puts the spotlight on Love Inspired Historical, with each book celebrating family and the special place it has in our hearts. Be sure to pick up all four Love Inspired Historical stories, available February 14, wherever books are sold.

Harlequin *Presents*®

USA TODAY bestselling author

Sarah Morgan

brings readers another enchanting story

ONCE A FERRARA WIFE...

When Laurel Ferrara is summoned back to Sicily by her estranged husband, billionaire Cristiano Ferrara, Laurel knows things are about to heat up. And Cristiano's power is a potent reminder of his Sicilian dynasty's unbreakable rule: once a Ferrara wife, always a Ferrara wife....

Sparks fly this February

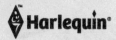
Harlequin®

n⬤cturne™